DISLOYALTY

"Be careful who you trust,

the devil was once an angel."

SHARI W. QUINN

Available on Kindle and other retail outlets

To order additional copies of this title, contact your favorite bookstore or visit www.shariquinn.com or email: info@shariquinn.com

Cover Design by Sterling A. McCollum

Cover Image Copyright © Elena Zharnova, 2013
Used under license from Shutterstock.com

Edited by Rob Brill and Shari W. Quinn
Interior Design by Shari W. Quinn

Printed in the United States of America
CreateSpace, Charleston, SC

ISBN: 0692214372

ISBN-13: 978-0692214374

To my children,

Sharia, Ruffus "Pop," and Malik

My prayer is that you each fulfill your purpose in life, pursue your dreams, and never stop until you reach them. You are in charge of your own destiny and are destined for greatness. In every reward and blessing you receive, be sure to find a positive way to pay it forward.

Let this book serve as a firm reminder that no matter with whom you are close, only put your faith and trust in Jesus Christ. Never will there be a more loyal and faithful friend than He.

Stay close to each other, motivate the other, for you are your sibling's keeper.

Keep reaching for the top!

All my love,
Mom

When I dare to be powerful –
to use my strength in the service of my vision,
then it becomes less and less important
whether I am afraid.

Audre Lorde

CONTENTS

acknowledgements

I would like to give a special thank-you to the wonderful woman who raised me, my mother, Ms. Willie B. Quinn. You have always been my biggest cheerleader and beside me every step of the way. You taught me to believe in myself, conquer challenges, and soar to great heights. Because of you, this past year I have learned the greatest amount of patience, humility, and the true meaning of sacrifice. Throughout my life, you have given me the world and unselfishly sacrificed yourself for your only child. Now it is my humble honor to sacrifice myself to aid you. I am eternally grateful for your unwavering love, support, and guidance.

I would also like to acknowledge my dearest uncle, mentor and friend, the late Hon. Nebraska O. Brace. You have always been one of my greatest supporters, encouragers and applauders. I know you are smiling down and happy to see another milestone achieved. If you were still walking this earth, I'm confident this book would be a best seller because you would carry it around in your inside jacket pocket telling the world about it, as you always did with each of my accomplishments. I am forever grateful for you and your inspiration. You were truly an icon and my hero. I pledge to honor your legacy and will continue your humanitarianism through the Hon. Nebraska O. Brace Scholarship Foundation.

barely innocent

Everyone has that one person they have great confidence in and deeply trust. For me, Gina was that person. We had been great friends for 20 years, and did so much together. Parties, after-work happy hours, vacations, family gatherings, happy or sad occasions, you name it — whatever it was, we were there. Where you saw one, you often saw the other. For the rare occasions we weren't out together, people would often ask the whereabouts of the other. No matter where we went or what we did, we were guaranteed a good time.

Our personalities complemented each other's. She and I were very different yet in sync. The synergy and harmony of the two of us walking in a room announced our arrival and magnified our presence. We had a sense of style and fashion, and we walked with a fierce, elegant thrust. My personality was more outgoing than Gina's shy nature. I was gregarious, energetic and a social butterfly. You could generally find me networking the room in my three-inch heels to heighten my five-two stature. With a wine glass in one hand, a napkin in the other, and my Fendi handbag tightly clutched under my arm, I'd move from one person to the next — smiling, talking, and nodding in agreement.

Gina, on the other hand, would quietly sit at the far corner of the bar texting on her cell phone or scrolling through Facebook while sparingly sipping on her tall margarita with Jose Cuervo, Grand Marnier, a twist of lime, and no salt. Two inches shorter than me, she'd sit at the bar as her short legs barely touched the ground and dangled from the bar stool like a child's legs suspended in the air on the Flying Swing at the local carnival. At the bar, she'd occasionally say hello to the person next to her and give a gentle wave or an unwelcoming smirk to someone passing by.

Although she and I were different in many ways, we shared a common bond of friendship, sisterhood, and loyalty. As sisters often do, we shared many secrets and personal experiences while offering guidance to the other. Because of my transparency and level of comfort, she was privy to my deepest secrets, desires, and concerns, and I felt safe sharing my vulnerability. Frankly, I thought the sentiment was mutual. Even though she was a quiet-natured person, I felt I knew the depth of her because of the history and length of our friendship. No matter how much I knew she was sneaky and deceptive, I interpreted her secretiveness as a need for privacy. I respected the boundaries and her space, and tried not to often pry into her private life.

Setting and respecting boundaries is essential in every healthy friendship or relationship. Although Gina and I hadn't clearly defined the parameters of our friendship, I made the dangerous mistake in assuming she respected the implied boundaries of our sisterhood. The guidelines were simple with basic rules of Girlfriend 101: Respect each other, honor confident conversations, and understand that the men we dated were off limits to the other. As women, I didn't think this was a conversation she and I needed to have considering we were both adults and longtime friends. I thought it was an automatic rule, but I was wrong.

I had no idea Gina had been sleeping with the man I was dating. Shocked and dumbfounded, I chose to ignore my initial suspicion because I couldn't imagine she would deliberately cross the dividing line. I also didn't want to accuse her of such a violation without being certain. Unbeknownst to me, Gina and Caleb's illicit affair went on for several months. Caleb and I had been dating for the past two years and up until the last three months, we had a nice relationship and a lot of fun together. We'd spent nearly every day together from the moment we met. He was a tall, thin, nice-looking man with dimples, squinty brown eyes, and short curly black hair.

While sitting in my living room chair, I waited for Caleb to come over from work as he did every day. I had just discovered he and Gina were sexually involved, and I was furious. I'd been sitting in the chair for an hour waiting and thinking what to say when he walked through the door. As soon as I heard the key enter the doorknob, I raced to the door, flung it open, and shouted in astonishment,

"Holy shit, Caleb! You've been fucking my best friend, Gina."

"What are you talking about? Are you serious?"

"Unbelievable! Of all people in the world, I would have never expected her to stab me in the back."

"Laila, you can't be serious. That half-pint dwarf-looking girl?"

"Caleb, please spare me. Please don't deflect and try to catalogue it by calling her out her name. Your reaction is so typical. This is your normal defense mechanism and reaction whenever you're wrong."

"Listen Laila, she's a nice girl and all, but I would never think of fooling around with her. She's not even cute, and honestly, she's not my fucking type."

"Pussy is your type."

After bursting into a laugh, he said, "You can't possibly be serious? She is not anyone I would be interested in. I don't deal with ugly chicks," he said as he continued laughing.

"I don't find anything funny about this."

"I'm not fucking your friend, Laila. Nobody is interested in that retarded-looking midget. I didn't need your friends before you, and I certainly don't need them now. Don't worry. You're safe with your whack-ass crew."

Caleb wasn't aware that I had suspected him and Gina of seeing each other behind my back. For the past two months, I'd watched and assessed their behavior, their movements, and their diligence in not getting caught. They both tried so hard to fool me but didn't realize that in every calculated move they made, they signaled clues of deception, and ultimately gave themselves away.

"You are so full of shit, Caleb. Little do you know, I saw your car parked near Gina's house late last night."

"You're mistaken because you did not see my car parked in front of Gina's. My car is in the shop. You always think you know something and are always blaming me for shit I haven't done," he said.

"You know what? You're right. I didn't see your car in front of Gina's, but I saw your aunt's car parked there. I already knew you borrowed your aunt's car while yours was in the shop, and you were parked at Gina's."

He looked shocked and stood in silence for a moment trying to think of something to say. He knew I was right, and knew I was aware of their inappropriate relationship. I had no other way of knowing he was parked near Gina's. If I hadn't seen it for myself, I would have believed him and apologized like a fool.

He wrecked his brain to figure out how I became aware of their affair after several months of sneaking behind my back. It was a vicious cycle to continue this conversation with Caleb because he never admitted the truth, so it was a pointless effort to convince him of honesty. Furthermore, I didn't necessarily need him to confess their relationship because I was unquestionably aware of their double-crossing.

everything comes to light

When it comes to my intuition, it's hard to fool me. I pretended to be clueless to allow additional time to carefully watch their actions. Their relationship was confirmed when I saw his aunt's car at Gina's house after midnight. Caleb didn't like to be wrong or questioned. He continued to rant, rave and ridicule Gina to give the impression that he wasn't interested in her. I'm very observant, and learned a lot just from watching him. After dealing with someone for two years, you learn their behavior patterns and know when they're not being honest. What's more, a woman's intuition alerts her when something isn't right. This was one of those situations and I had enough.

I often knew when Caleb was lying, but I picked my battles and let him think he was fooling me. Besides, he had no idea his Aunt Lilly secretly told me he was fooling around with Gina, and that I needed to watch her. I never said anything to Caleb or Gina about their indiscretion because I didn't want to compromise

Aunt Lilly's trust. She was a sweet little woman in her mid-60's whom I completely adored. She was 4 foot 11 and stocky but a real powerhouse. There was no messing around with Aunt Lilly. She was a straight shooter and didn't tolerate nonsense. She spoke out on what's right, had no problem telling you if you were wrong, and didn't bite her tongue. She even matter-of-factly told me on a few occasions I needed to leave her cold-hearted selfish nephew and find a more decent man. She was right, but I refused to listen.

Aunt Lilly and I became close after meeting at a family wedding. She regularly invited me to her home for her famous blueberry cornbread muffins and rum mudslides. It was an interesting combination but rather delightful. While enjoying her company, we would sit and talk for hours in her all-white living room with mirrored walls. She showed me cute baby pictures of Caleb, shared funny stories of him growing up, but more importantly gave me words of wisdom and encouragement to release Caleb. She was compelled to remind me that Caleb and Gina were both deceiving me, and didn't want to me remain in the dark.

My relationship with him was on its last leg and it became extremely toxic. We went back and forth multiple times, and it seemed like we never allowed each other to close the relationship. We'd spent the last three months arguing and bickering, but sadly neither of us would let go. We stayed in the unhealthy relationship and drove each other crazy. Just a week earlier, he and I had a heated argument. He got so belligerent. In his effort to pick a fight with me, he

8

blurted out, "That's why one of your friends made sexual advances toward me."

"Ok, that's great!" I said as if I didn't care. "And why do you feel the need to tell me this now, Caleb?"

He chuckled and said, "They laugh in your face too."

"Well, it doesn't matter because as I told you Gina is the only one I consider a true friend, so if someone made sexual advances toward you, then have at it. I don't care."

"She's a lil' sexy sneaky bitch too," he said.

"OK, that's great, Caleb," I said once again as if I didn't care, but I was shocked he implied Gina had been suggestive toward him. I dismissed it because I was confident of her unwavering loyalty. He later claimed he was joking and there was "nothing sexy about her," but I knew it was another one of his tactics to distract my attention from their hot-and-steamy affair. There wasn't a need for him to defend it. I knew the truth and didn't even plan to mention their fling to Gina. I intended to play along and just allow Karma to bite her in the ass.

I was done with the conversion, but apparently he wasn't. He went on and on for the next several hours as he tried to feel me out to get an idea of what I thought about this, but I played it cool. I knew it was only a matter of time before I caught them myself. During the next six-hour saga of him playing his normal manipulative mind games, he managed to get a hold of Tabatha to have her call me.

Tabatha was the third wheel to Gina and me, and was more Gina's friend than mine. They grew up together, had worked together many years ago as orderlies at the local hospital, and remained close. Before Tabatha and I connected, Gina would often mention Tabatha's name, but I had no clue who she was. Even though we grew up in the same small town and went to the same high school, I'd never heard of her before. From Gina's description of her, I thought she was a local newspaper journalist because she knew almost everything that went on in town and everyone's personal business. Turned out, she was just a nosy person, a busybody and a meddler who just couldn't help herself. I should have known she was nothing but trouble.

Despite Gina's perception of her, I suggested she invite Tabatha to accompany us on our evening excursion. Gina was extremely apprehensive because of Tabatha's poor fashion sense and didn't want to be embarrassed by her lack of style, and inelegant and unpolished behavior. Tabatha, insecure about her radiant dark midnight skin, was a tomboy who wore construction boots and Air Jordan's with sweat pants and hooded sweat jackets. This was embarrassing to Gina since she and I generally wore fashionable cocktail dresses and stiletto heels, and clutched our evening handbags. I told Gina to stop being so mean and invite Tabatha, and suggested we assist her in selecting something nice to wear. After tugging with

Gina for a week, she obliged and invited her friend. It didn't matter to me one way or another if she went, but I thought it would be a nice gesture to get her out the house since Gina mentioned Tabby had been depressed since her live-in boyfriend started a new family with an older woman across town.

To put Tabatha's place in the friendship circle into perspective, before she became the third wheel there was always Gina, myself and another girlfriend who later moved out of state. Now I will be honest in saying, the three of us were the center of attention when we walked in a room with all eyes were on us. It had been that way for many years, really because of the other girlfriend and me, but Gina eventually elevated to our level. When our mutual friend moved out of the area there essentially was an opening, and we made her audition for the role and reluctantly accepted her in.

Caleb got a hold of Tabatha through Gina when I was flipping out about their sexual affair. While I ran to the store, they got on a three-way call and Caleb explained my accusations. From there, Tabatha came up with the bright idea to suggest that she call me saying Caleb called her cellphone looking for Gina to talk to me about my insinuations. Tabby was a criminal-minded and on-your-toes thinker who could swiftly create the world's greatest and most convincing lie just from the inflection in her tone of voice and by swearing on her loved one's grave or her life. Her performance was compelling and award-winning.

First, I received a text message on my iPhone from

Tabby, saying, "Hey girl, call me right away, Caleb just called my phone asking for Gina."

Playing along with their game I replied, "Oh my God, he is too much. I'm calling you right now. Are you at work?"

"Yes"

"OK," I typed in my response.

I knew she was lying as she always did because I purposely sent her and Gina a text earlier that day that I knew who Caleb was sneaking around with. Gina never replied to my text, but Tabby asked in her reply, "Oh my God, who is it, Arnell?"

Tabatha and Gina were crafty liars. I knew damn well it wasn't Arnell, even though, she too, turned out to be shady. Tabby also mentioned in her text that Gina wanted me to know she left her cell phone at home and would call me later when she ran home on lunch to get it, which I knew was a load of malarkey. If you didn't intrinsically know Tabby, you would be subject to believe her creative lies. There wasn't anything about her that took me by surprise.

Gina's two-timing actions, however, very much surprised me. She and I been friends for over two decades and I could never understand why she chose to betray me, especially with corny-ass Caleb. I once heard she was sleeping with a past boyfriend of mine but I didn't believe it at first. Part of me also didn't care because he was a large, bald butterball with glasses whom I cared nothing about. I did, however, care about Caleb, and could never fathom how he became of interest to her. She was a seemingly sweet, angelic person with the most annoying childlike voice who consistently portrayed the innocent girl image and was anything but. Although she was sneaky, we never had a disagreement or argument, and got along very well. She was nonjudgmental and supportive of me and my endeavors until I later found out from Tabby that she was in fact judgmental towards me and my various community-service and professional pursuits. I also wasn't aware until Tabby shared Gina was envious of me, and intimidated by my success and popularity. People had always told me that, including our other girlfriend, but I never saw it. I wrecked my brain to figure out what caused her to stab me in the back.

Her betrayal and deception deeply wounded me, and the pain was immeasurable. She knew me well, and should have known it would only be a matter of time before I pieced together the puzzle of their deceit. I was more hurt by Gina than I was by Caleb's deception. Men will be men, and this was to be expected of Caleb because he had no sense of loyalty to anyone. He was selfish and all about rising to the top at the expense of someone else, but I didn't expect this from Gina.

In my distress, I knew I would eventually get over the ordeal because he wasn't worth my well-being or my time. He was a scumbag and a manipulative creep who charmed the pants off my weak girlfriend. But for Gina, he was the best thing she could get since there weren't many available men who were romantically interested in her. I scrolled through the history of our text messages in my phone. I was further disturbed to discover the number of times she'd manipulated me in her quest to find out my whereabouts in order to hook up with Caleb. On 22 separate occasions, she invited me to her cluttered second-floor apartment. The purpose of her invitation wasn't ever truly for dinner but for me to advise her when I was leaving my home 30 minutes away and to announce my arrival to allow the two of them time in bed before he rushed out her back door.

He was right about one thing: She was very sneaky. Another 17 times she sent me a text message indicating she had just seen him near her house 30 miles away and three cities over, and another nine times she saw him driving home or ran into him at various locations in her small, former mill village area. Routinely she called to tell me about other women interested in him, women posting on his Facebook page and sent me screenshots of posts as a distraction. All of her actions were conniving, calculating, and cunning — and a lie. To some extent she was honest in saying she seen him, but failed to mention it was in her cramped dull bedroom.

It was peculiar the many times she claimed to run into him. We are all from the same small town and in my 40 years, I never ran into him. In fact, I hadn't run into him in the six months since our breakup. No matter how much a person tries to hide deceit, life has a way of letting things come to light. The sad part is although the light brightly cascaded over Gina, she continued the secret love affair without any remorse, guilt, or shame. For a person to look you straight in your face, smile and laugh knowing they are dishonest is mortifying. Her actions validated she was a cold-hearted, venomous snake.

I was embarrassed, and consumed by hurt. I felt as though I was the biggest fool to have that much faith and trust in a friend. Part of the hurt and embarrassment was because I had been in the dark for many months. Their fling went on right under my nose and I had no idea. I would have sworn on my life that she would never do anything like this.

Often I hosted dinner parties at my home with the two of them present, and was in the dark about them playing footsies under my table and sneaking in my bathroom while I was outside grilling lobsters. Three separate times, they arrived at my dinner parties five minutes behind the other after just leaving her house, and walked into mine smiling and laughing, and sat at my dinner table while I served them gourmet meals.

They both are sick individuals without morals, values or principles but deserve each other. Caleb had such a stronghold on Gina and manipulated her into believing he truly cared about her. She should have questioned his motives because no one other than one of her child's fathers had ever cared about her but she was fascinated by the thrill of sneaking even though she was concurrently seeing other unavailable men. While sneaking around with Caleb, she was dealing with a married man for 10 years as well as one of her co-workers, one of the local corrupt police officers, and a laborer originally from West Africa.

She had always quietly been this way which explains why people found it hard to believe she would stab me in the back but they didn't know her true character as I did. I wasn't surprised when she divulged to me that she didn't know the true identity of one of her kid's fathers. Even though the child has asked her about it, Gina denied it and refused to get a paternity test in fear of the truth. She had misled her family and child for many years so surely she would deceive me. In spite of this, she dealt with Caleb as well as the other men at the same time, all unprotected. These thrilling escapades come with a price, and could cost you your health, dignity, and friendships, none of which she treasured.

She was so busy scheming and betraying me, and monitoring my whereabouts she failed to calculate the cost of our longtime sisterhood. With Caleb as a variable in the equation, their love affair will equal chaos, confusion, and destruction.

created conflict

Gina was not certain that I was aware of her relationship with Caleb. I'd been on to them for the last two months but hadn't said a word to her about it. We spoke several times a day but I didn't bother saying anything. Instead, I gave her several opportunities during our conversations to voluntarily confess. I wanted to see how long she'd continue the pretentiousness of smiling and laughing in my face, whine dining at my dinner table and clinging wine glasses as we sipped sparkling white wine.

"What are we toasting to? The fact that two best friends are sharing the same man? How long can a person continue this charade and it not affect their conscious?" were questions I asked myself. I couldn't remain silent to their fling any longer. I carefully thought about the best way to objectively approach her about this without involving my emotions or without the conversation getting out of control. Because my frustration was growing, she began to sense I was on to her so she closely gauged my behavior around her to conclude if I knew about their disloyal affair or not.

There were so many ways I wanted to address this and came up with the idea of inviting her to lunch. There was a new Irish sports bar near her job that she and I went to a few times for happy hour. It was nearby and a great location to have a private conversation without a large crowd. I intended to have a straightforward nonthreatening discussion with her but remembered she's not the type to confess her wrongdoings or admit guilt because she's the type to take her dirt to her grave. Whether she confessed or not, chances were the lunch probably would have ended with me slapping her across her face. Therefore, meeting for lunch was not a good idea. I would have landed in the county lock-up after she called the police, and she would have also called her other secret lover, the local police officer to have him further pursue the charges. I tried to think of another approach to talk with her. I sat on my living room floor going through 20 years of photos of Gina and me. It seemed as if I were going through a terrible breakup with a boyfriend as I reminisced and looked at the memories we shared. As I turned each page of the vacation photo albums, I'd sipped my glass of Red Moscato and sobbed. Pictures of the two of us smiling, posing and enjoying life. Pictures with the kids and others at various gatherings. The more I sipped my wine and turned the plastic photo pages, the more the tears rolled down my face, and I uncontrollably cried.

"Damn you, Gina," I said as I slapped the photo album. I was crushed. I violently ripped up our photos straight down the middle between the images of her and me. I thought each photo rip would ease the pain of her betrayal, but it didn't help. Grabbing my glass of wine, I stopped destroying the photos and came up with the creative idea of making her a photo collage of our 20 years together so she could see the damage she did to our friendship.

The next four hours, I spent sorting through decades of albums from our yearly vacations and everyday snapshots. There were memorable photos from our trips to Puerto Rico, the Bahamas, Chicago, Las Vegas, New York City, and Atlanta. Some of the other photo albums stored pictures from my wedding, baby showers, family funerals, our kids' birthday parties, Super Bowl parties, and our individual birthday celebrations. I removed 30 pictures from the albums that spanned over 20 years and took them to the local CVS photo kiosk to design and print a beautiful leather-bound album with our picture embedded as a gift for her — and to see her reaction. If she could view all the wonderful moments in our sisterhood without emotion, it would further confirm her cold-heart. Lucky for her, I didn't get to make the photo album since so many people in the store had the similar Christmas gift idea.

Instead, I went to pay her a surprise visit at her job to bring her an early Christmas present since it was Christmas Eve. As expected, she was shocked to see me because during the 10 years she worked there, I had never visited her on the job. She often said I had impulsive violent actions. I'm sure this is partly what caused her face to turn beat red when I walked in the door. She wasn't expecting me and didn't know why I was there. To keep her composure, she looked me in my eyes and tried to maintain a straight face while acting happy to see me. It was a poor performance.

She tried to play it cool since Caleb schooled her on acting tough. He told her what I said about me being at her house a few nights prior for our annual Christmas gift exchange dinner, and her not being able to look me in my face because she sensed I was aware of their affair. So he prepared her for the possibility of her and I being in each other's company again. I knew her better than anyone, and knew her behavior was just a game. Her conversation was fake, and so were her smiles. We didn't have our normal, "Hey girl, good to see you" greeting or conversation. It was very bland, phony, and forced.

To break the ice and ease her discomfort of my presence, I handed her a gift card to her favorite chain restaurant and a special Christmas card that read:

> To Gina: My dearest friend,
>
> Words cannot express
> How it feels to have
> such a friend like you.
> If only we could trade places
> for just a single moment,
> then you will know
> how it feels
> to have such

a friend like you.

Lots of love,
Laila

I couldn't believe I found the perfect card that articulated my exact sentiments. The words were priceless and true because if she and I could have traded places for just a moment, she would have self-awareness to see what an awful friend she had been. It was truly a Hallmark moment. To my surprise, she didn't seem moved or touched by my card. The fact I was still at her office could have attributed to her unaffected reaction. She read it with a straight face, if she even read it all. I promise, if I wasn't being considered for a career promotion, I would have snatched her over the counter by her ponytail and dragged her out the door.

I don't believe I'd ever been so angry with a person. To be sure she read it, I made her read it out loud. I forgot she had reading challenges and later remembered she was a special education student on the short yellow bus when we were in middle school, and later went to the alternative high school because the rigorous curriculum was too overwhelming for her. But she quickly read the card, closed it, and sarcastically thanked me. I told her I had more gifts and would stop by her house later that evening.

I didn't have any more gifts for her because I gave all her Christmas presents away once I learned of her betrayal. I just told her I was coming by to see the reaction I would get from her and have her on edge a bit. I also knew she would try to keep Caleb away that evening since she thought I might stop by. I called her a few hours later that evening but conveniently she wasn't home. A couple hours later, she texted me that she just returned home and was sorry she missed me."

"No problem, I'm actually not too far away from you so I'll stop by shortly," I replied.

Thirty-minutes later, she replied, "OK, sounds good. See you soon."

I had no intentions of going to her house. In fact, I was already home in bed, but I got up because I had another brilliant idea. I created a beautiful video online photo slideshow of our pictures using a photo app from my smartphone. I used the pictures that I'd planned to incorporate into the photo album at CVS. The app was sophisticated and robust, allowing users to customize the slideshow with their favorite music as well. So I set the background music to our girlfriend-theme-song "Best Friend" by Brandy. Years ago when we were much younger, we used to have the song set as each other's ringtone. The video was titled, "20 Years of Sisterhood." It was well designed and came out very nice. I posted the photo slideshow on Facebook and tagged her in the post for our accumulative 2,300 friends to view in their timelines. Within minutes, it went from one like to 179 likes. Our collective friends posted their comments to the video.

"True sisterhood."

"Good friendships are hard to find."

"All this time I thought you two were blood sisters."

"Love and loyalty. That's family right there," her nephew posted.

"I always have a ball of fun with you two. I can't wait until we hang out again," her older cousin wrote.

"Awhh, this is so sweet and special. Good friends are hard to find."

"You guys are always together. Great friends."

"Two beautiful ladies, love the video."

"Friendship, sisterhood and loyalty."

Over 63 comments were posted with people sharing their sentiments about friendship and loyalty. Gina had the nerve to like every comment someone posted and disingenuously commented in agreement on each one.

"Thank you for your comment. I am so thankful to have her as my dear friend."

"She is such a dear friend, I don't know what I would do without her," she posted.

Her sarcasm infuriated me. I knew Caleb was behind the scenes coaching her once again to comment because she's not that bright or brave, and she wouldn't independently think to comment on her own. He knew how to get under my skin and always liked to prod at people to annoy them. He was the master of pissing me off, and she became his little string puppet.

Alerts and notifications from Facebook appeared on my phone screen indicating there were additional comments and likes from our mutual friends — and her. Each time someone posted on the video, she'd immediately clicked the like button, one by one. Each time I received a notification indicating she liked it, I became more furious. Clearly, she and Caleb were having a good time at my expense and thought her commenting was funny. However, I was not amused so I sent her a text message.

"Hey Gina, I haven't heard from you in a couple days. We usually talk every day. I'm really surprised at you and have been waiting for you to come clean with me about your indiscretion. I considered you my sister, and even though I have my own blood sisters, it was you who I called to meet me at the hospital when my cousin died. I would love to hear from you."

Several minutes passed without a reply from her. I waited a few more minutes until I decided to pick up the phone to call her.

"Hello," she politely answered.

"Hey Gina."

"Oh, hey Laila, I was just about to call you."

"Really? I was wondering why I hadn't heard from you. What's going on?"

"Well, I was going to ask you the same thing because you've been acting very weird toward me lately."

"Weird? I told you a few days ago, I've been going through a lot. My aunt is in the hospital, my grandmother isn't feeling well and I've been dealing with my own personal issues."

"Yes, I understand that. But you've been acting funny toward me," she said in her childlike whiny voice. "Well, I'm just going to tell you what I heard."

"Tell me what, Gina?"

"Well, when we went skiing the other day, my babe told me he overheard that you think I'm fucking with Caleb."

"Oh, really? Your babe told you that? Then why don't we get your babe's wife on the phone to speak to him so we can find out if he truly told you that?"

"Now Laila, why would you do that?"

"Because you're a fucking liar. Caleb told you to say that, and he's also the one who told you about my suspicions."

"Laila, I can't believe you would think I would mess around with him. We've been friends for a long time and I would never do that to you. I swear on my grandparent's grave."

"Oh shut up, Gina, that means nothing to you. You used them anyway."

"I beg your pardon? Laila, I can't believe you would say that to me; and I can't believe you would think I would be involved with him. First it was Tabatha, now me."

"Tabatha?"

"Yea, you said Tabatha was messing with one of your friends a couple of years ago."

"I never said nor implied that about Tabatha."

"You did, and now you think it's me. You know what? We've been friends for 20 years and it's been real. You fucked up our 20-year friendship. You take care of yourself."

"What? Are you kidding me? If you're not fooling around with him then why are you so defensive and upset? I think you're saying all of this because you know you're caught. Why don't you just meet me somewhere tonight?"

"Meet you? Meet for what?"

"Do you have a problem with meeting me?"

"Well, I've been drinking, it's late and I have to finish wrapping Christmas presents. I don't want drink and drive, and you're not thinking clearly right now. I know how crazy you are and that you hear voices in your head?"

"What? Regina Renee? Really? I know Caleb told you to say that as well. What is wrong with you? That's some foolishness he had you say to get under my skin. I can't believe you're not taking responsibility for your actions."

"I'm not messing around with corny-ass Caleb."

"You are so full of it, Gina."

"Ok, I'm fine with that. Whatever. You're crazy."

"You know what? You're taking this somewhere it doesn't have to go. I can see the headline on the 11 o'clock news now, "Two Best Friends ...""

"Sounds good! Do what you gotta do, baby," she said as she tried to raise her juvenile voice.

I slammed the phone and hung up. I couldn't believe she deflected the situation and didn't take responsibility for her actions.

"All over this worthless man?" I asked myself. "How did he get to her like that and so fast?"

She allowed this manipulative joker to come between our friendship. He cared more about his animals than anyone human on earth, and he certainly didn't care about the friendship between Gina and me. Thirty minutes later I received a call from Landan, whom was well known as LJ. He was a mutual friend of ours who was always the sole guy accompanying us girlfriends.

Landan and I knew each other since we were kids, and our grandmothers were very good friends. From a young age, he was reared by his Italian godfather, Nino, who was a ruthless mobster with ties to a large organized crime family. I knew Landan much longer than I knew Gina and Tabatha combined. In fact, he and I dated many years ago, and maintained a very close friendship over the years. Gina and Tabatha were the only two who knew of my history with Landan. He visited my home a couple of occasions in Philly, and felt rejected when I escorted him out of my spacious master bedroom suite to sleep in the adjacent guest room. The past three years since I'd been back in Charleston, he pretended to be close to me, referred to me as his sister, and cock-blocked everyone I considered dating. Gina often said he regularly hung around us because he still wanted me which explained why he always found something wrong with anyone I dated. No one seemed good enough whenever I asked his opinion. Although we eventually formed a pseudo brother-sister relationship, he was still salty with me about the rejection.

"Hey LJ, what's up?"

"Caleb asked me to call you. He wanted me to talk to you. I told him I wasn't getting involved and was going to stay out of it, but he insisted I call you because he said you think he's messing around with Gina."

"Well it's a good thing you said you didn't want to get involved because I really don't want to talk to you about it."

"He just wanted me to let you know that you're bugging and nothing is going on between them."

"He's a fucking liar, and so is she."

"You're bugging, that's your girl."

"She's not my girl. She was just on the phone talking shit to me, and had the nerve to say her babe told her he overheard that I thought she was fucking with Caleb. She's a liar."

"You know what? I told her to say that. She didn't want to say I told her, so she said her babe."

I knew Landan was lying because I've been around him when he told similar lies to other people. He long ago proved himself as untrustworthy. Besides, he wasn't making any sense. I just pretended to listen as I shook my head on the phone, and thought, "How worse can this call get?" They're all lying to me and covering for each other. "And these are my friends?" I asked myself.

He continued, "You know Gina better than anyone. She wouldn't do that to you."

"You're absolutely right. I do know Gina better

than anyone and although I would have never expected her to do this to me, this is certainly her character. For nearly the 20 years I have known her, she has always been sneaky and screwed around someone else's man or husband. Besides, a reliable source told me about her and Caleb today."

"A reliable source?"

"Yes, a very reliable source."

"More reliable than your girl? You're going to put someone else's word above your girl's? Where's your loyalty?"

"Loyalty? Are you kidding me? I've been more than a friend to her for years. More importantly, I valued her, viewed her as my sister, and she stabbed me in the back. She was conniving and sneaky, monitoring my moves and calculating her steps to make sure the coast was clear to sneak around with him. Besides, I know for a fact she's been fucking him. I've known for a while and have been trying to catch them myself. And like I said, someone very reliable told me today."

"So what? Even if she did, so what?"

"So what? I'm sorry, but I expect more from my friendships."

"You're going to throw 20 years of friendship down the drain for some dick? Men come and go. Fuck Caleb, Gina's your best friend."

"With friends like that, who needs enemies?"

"You're really being unreasonable right now. You know I love you. We're like family, but I'm beginning to think you're crazy like everyone's been saying."

"Well, if you think I'm crazy, then you don't have to speak to me either. I could care less. None of ya'll have to speak to me."

"You're just going to isolate yourself like that from your friends?"

"There's a distinct difference between isolation, and choosing not to be around phony people. Trust me, I know many people, can meet new people, and will have no problem surrounding myself with sea of positive people."

"Laila, I can't believe you right now."

"The moment she slipped and fell on his dick was the moment our friendship ended. Fuck her. I really don't want to talk about this any longer. This conversation is pointless. I don't want to hang up on you, but I have to go."

I knew Landan was full of it and also knew Caleb didn't ask him to call me. He inserted himself into the equation as he always has to give the impression he was the peacemaker and the level-headed person, but I knew better.

pose as a friend

I didn't expect to wake up at 5 a.m. but got up to take a few ibuprofens for my headache. I was surprised to get a phone call from Tabatha so early in the morning. We spoke regularly in the mornings but never that early.

"Hey girl, good morning. Is everything OK?"

"Hey, listen, Laila, I wish we could really fix this."

"Are you crying, Tabby?"

"This is going too far, and I care about the both of ya'll. We have to fix this. Thing is just wrong."

"What's just wrong? What are you talking about?"

"Since you said you guys are going to headline on the 11 o'clock news, they called Gina's uncle to get involved. They were all yelling in the background and talking about fighting."

"Are you serious? They are so immature. We are

in our 40's? Who does that?"

"We just have to fix this. Can't we all just sit down and talk about it?"

"Well, there's no fixing it, Tabby, so you can stop crying. All good things come to an end, and we've reached the end of our friendship."

"We've all been friends for so long. I can't believe you guys are going to let 20 years of friendship go down the drain. It's almost like a marriage. This just doesn't affect you and Gina, it affects all of us, our friends, our family."

"It's not that serious, Tabby."

"What are you guys going to say when each of your family members asks about the other? This just isn't right."

Tabatha seemed very upset and emotional. She was hysterically crying on the phone. Gina and I weren't breaking a sweat about it, so I was not sure why everyone else seemed interested. Tabatha insisted Gina and I try to talk about the broken friendship and make amends. She blamed Caleb for this confusion and chaos, as she continued to cry.

"I wish you never met him. He is a very dangerous and manipulative man. If he didn't come into your life, none of this would have happened. He's just not a good person. You have to be careful of who you let come into your life."

"What do you mean by that?"

"Listen, you're very intelligent and can put things together, just as I put it together that his aunt Lilly told you about him and Gina."

"I'm listening."

"He came into your life at a vulnerable time when your cousin died; he came into your life for a purpose. And it wasn't for good intentions."

"I'm not sure where you're going with this?"

"When you let negative people into your life, confusion follows, and look at what he did. He is evil. A few months ago, you said the psychic said you were going to be financially set beginning in December, you would reconnect with a former male friend in the spring, and next year was going to be a prosperous one for you. Maybe you should go back to the psychic to see what she has to say, and see if she has anything new to tell you."

With Tabatha telling me to read between the lines, it sounded like she knew of my grave fate that varied from the psychic's optimistic reading. There was an awkward silence over the phone. I knew what she was trying to tell me but waited for her to finish her story.

Finally, she said, "Listen, Laila, I probably shouldn't tell you this, but I'm going to because this has gone too far and you need to know."

"Know what?"

"Caleb was hired by Brent and LJ to date you."

"What?!"

"You heard me. A while back LJ told Brent it was you who smashed his windows, and told Brent to tell you the flashing camera in the traffic light caught you on film. He thought ratting you out would help him get the job with Brent's friend but unbeknownst to him Brent already told his friend not to hire him."

"Unreal"

"You have to be careful who you let into your life. Even though you paid Brent restitution, he never got over what you did to his house and store windows or how you had him crying to everyone. He has been trying to get back at you for the last three years."

"Are you serious?"

"Yes, Brent has been plotting against you for a while."

"When your cousin recently passed away, he and LJ figured this was a good time to have someone come into your life to lure you with compassion. LJ introduced Brent to Caleb."

"Holy shit! What kind of craziness is that? This sounds like a movie."

"Yes it does. I have never heard of such craziness

either. When you and Caleb first started dating, Caleb made several attempts to harm you but always missed the opportunity."

I was shocked by what Tabatha told me. I wasn't shocked by Brent or Landan because I knew their characters and both were good as posing as friends. I was, however, surprised by Caleb because he seemed very much into me, was around me all the time and seemingly had a vested interest, or at least that's what I thought. If what she said was true, he was very good at playing the role.

She continued, "Brent and LJ told him you have a violent temper and when upset you might try to put your hands on him, and since he's nice with his hands he would knock you out."

"I think I've heard enough."

"Wait, listen. You need to hear this. He planned to push you off the cliff when you guys when hiking, but you got scared and never went to the top of the mountain. Another time, he tried to get you around someone who had a hit on them so it would look like you were an innocent bystander.

"Unbelievable!"

"He even made a copy of your car keys and planned to snip all the wires underneath the hood of your car so your vehicle would be inoperable. He talked about pulling the pin from your steering axel to make you dangerously lose control while driving."

"Whoa!"

"Girl, he is crazy, and he's obsessed with trying to hurt you. He even sabotaged a photo shoot you had scheduled. He told Gina all of this. He even planned to loosen the lug nuts on your tires so your wheels would fall off when you accelerated onto the highway to cause you grave danger. He actually tried that twice. Each time you got in the way of his plan."

"Sounds more like God got in the way."

"After months of you guys spending time together and him being around you all the time, he got to know the real you which differed from how you were perceived. He saw you were really sweet and not how Brent and LJ portrayed you. He developed a keen interest in you and had strong feelings for you until you recently pulled the knife on him. He's really upset about that."

"I didn't pull a knife on him. He's such a liar."

"Let me finish. Apparently you met a guy few weeks ago at your aunt's birthday party, but he was really Caleb's friend from the military. They set you up. Caleb knew you were trying to get out the house more since you two stopped seeing each other. He had his friend pretend to like you, and eventually get you in a comfortable place and stab you to death."

"What in the world?"

"That's why I've been crying all night and this

morning. This is going to way too far. I've been trying to calm everyone down because they're plotting to really hurt you or kill you. They're trying to make it appear as Gina's ex and uncle are responsible since you and Gina have been arguing. They knew you would have your family go after Gina's ex and family, but it's really Brent, Caleb and LJ."

"That's sick."

"Yeah, it really is. I feel I'm in middle. I love both you guys, and I don't want to see anything happen to either of you. I told LJ last night this was too much, it's going too far, and I can't take it. He told me to stop being a fucking punk and suck it up."

"Unbelievable."

the grocery store

After my four-hour phone call with Tabatha, the day went downhill from there. It was a day filled with turmoil, chaos, and disbelief. It was getting late and dark, and I was tired. I was driving all evening, from town to town thinking. My eyes were heavy. I could barely keep them open. Aimlessly, I drove while trying to figure out where I was going to sleep because I was too frightened to go home. The people I knew as my friends had come to my house earlier that day to cause trouble with me, and intended to return to my house to pay me another surprise visit and catch me off guard.

I couldn't believe I considered them actual friends of mine, or how I ended up with such friends. I tried to make sense of the day, but it made no sense at all. I didn't understand how it went terribly wrong or how it came to the point of planned violence, but I shouldn't have been surprised because they don't think rationally or maturely. I knew better than to remain friends with them. I reflected on my friendship with Tabatha, Gina, and LJ, and recalled how my instincts nudged me when I first moved back to the area to distance myself from them. I knew I outgrew the friendships a long time ago. We didn't have anything in common. Professionally and socially, we were all just unalike. Our conversations, values, interests, and goals were no longer parallel but for the sake of bonds and longevity I remained. Besides, it wasn't necessarily a big deal considering I wasn't around them much. I lived a thousand miles away in Philadelphia prior to moving back to Charleston, South Carolina, and only saw them once a year for a few days. I should have heeded to my instincts and parted from them. This was a very big lesson on following your instincts.

I continued to drive and ponder where I should stay for the night. I knew they were still trying to catch up to me because Tabatha called and texted me numerous times to track me down. I ignored her calls, messages, and voicemails. Going to my grandmother's house was not a viable option considering they knew where she lived and would go there too. They also would expect me to go to my mother's. I needed to do the opposite. They also knew my aunt's house or goddaughter's were another option so I didn't want to go to their homes either. Going to the obvious places would be a trap. I had to stay a few steps ahead of them.

My options were running out when I drove into the deserted parking lot of the Super 8 motel, along State Highway 64. A red fluorescent vacancy sign flashed against the smeared window. I sat in my car trying to decide whether I should go in or continue to the house of an old friend whom I have known for 25 years. She was not a friend of Gina's or Tabatha's, and neither knew anything about her. However, she lived with her family. I didn't want to bring this type of drama to their home. Although I'd been confiding in her about the drama details surrounding Gina, Tabatha, and Caleb, I didn't want to involve her and her family in this spectacle.

After 15 minutes of watching cars pull in and out of the motel parking lot, I grabbed my overstuffed Louis Vuitton duffle bag from my trunk and struggled to carry the heavy bag inside. I walked in the small lobby that was filled with the stench of mildew. I couldn't put my hand over my nose because I was carrying my heavy overnight bag with both hands to prevent the bulging clothes from falling on the floor. When I got to the counter, I dropped the bag in relief, handed my driver's license and credit card to the slim Middle Eastern hotel clerk.

"Can I get a room for one night, please?"

"For one person?"

"Yes, it's just me. I'll need a late checkout as well."

"OK. I'll just need to gather some information from you. Please fill out the registration card."

She slid a pen and an index-card size registration form across the counter. I filled out my name, address, make and model of my car, and license plate information, and slid it back to her. She slowly punched my information into the slow-processing computer using two fingers. I was already frustrated and tired, and her inability to type was going to take a while. After she inputted my information, she slid my credit card through the processing machine. I noticed she ran the card through the machine more than once.

"Is there a problem?" I asked.

"I'm sorry, your credit card was declined. Do you have another form of payment?"

"Oh, goodness, I just used this card 10 minutes ago at the gas station."

"I don't what to say. It's not working."

"OK, here's another one."

We tried two other credit cards, both were declined, and they didn't accept cash without a valid credit card on file to hold the charges. I snatched my duffle bag off the floor, headed back to the car and plopped my stuff on the front passenger seat. I was tired as hell with nowhere to go. I needed a moment to think this through and needed to take a break from driving. A half a mile down the road, I pulled into the 24-hour grocery store parking lot.

I felt I was running out of options and thought of a couple of friends who lived out of the Charleston area — in Columbia, South Carolina; Augusta, Georgia; Florida, and New York City. Since Columbia was less than a two-hour drive on I-26, I sent my friend a text and asked if he would open his doors to me for a few days while I figured out my next move. My friend in Columbia was a single dad who shared custody with his ex-wife. He was very welcoming and invited me stay but wanted me to know his two teenage children were still there for the next three days. I didn't want to go to his house with the kids there nor bunk with two potentially snotty teenagers. I also didn't want to wait three days or stay in the Charleston area.

I was exhausted, restless, and frantic. I had been awake since three o'clock in the morning, I'd been driving around since 3:15 in the afternoon, and it was now after nine at night. I sat in the grocery store parking lot for another hour and drifted off to sleep. I caught myself nodding off several times but forced myself to stay awake because the phrase "never let 'em catch you sleeping" replayed over and over in my mind. Although it's a figurative expression, I took it literally for the moment and instinctively knew something was not right. I needed to stay alert but couldn't stay in the parking lot much longer.

Using my iPhone, I searched the Internet for phone numbers to women's shelters, domestic violence houses, and safe houses. I had a difficult time getting through to the first three centers listed. While making a call to the fourth place, I noticed in my rearview mirror an older model black Acura coupe with two young people in it slowly drive past the back of my car. Not once, but three times within a minute and a half. The third time, the young male driver crept up to my car to read my distinctive car tag. I became suspicious and worried about the pair in the vehicle.

After they read my license plate, the driver raced to the side of the grocery store building and disappeared toward the rear. I continued to make my calls but something did not feel right so I decided to leave. I drove to the side parking lot and noticed the black Acura tucked along the side of the building with its lights off. The youngsters in the car noticed me, made eye contact and slid down in their seats to avoid being recognized. My hunch was right about them. They were up to something. Whether or not it had anything to do with me, I knew I needed to leave. As I approached the exit, they drove behind me with their car lights still off.

To test my theory of them following me, I slowly veered to the right toward the grocery store parking lot instead of exiting. As I suspected, they too made a right turn and proceeded behind me. After another 450 feet, I took a left turn near the other side of the store and watched them in my rearview mirror as they made the same turn. When they realized I was aware of them, they sped off but reappeared in two minutes. I drove to a well-lit area, parked among the commotion on the busier side of the parking lot.

Many cars came in and out of the lot. I never realized so many people went to the grocery so late at night. As I sat there, another suspicious looking white Ford F-150 pickup with a thunderous muffler sound drove up. Its driver also stopped to read my rear license plate. I yanked my gear shift into drive and drove to a different area of the parking lot. I would have driven off, but since I wasn't familiar with that part of town, I decided to stay nearby in the well-lit busy parking lot. Both vehicles stayed close by. The Acura drove toward the back of my car, the F-150 truck in front, aiming to block me in. With little time to spare, I raced to the front of the 24-hour grocery store, slammed on my brakes, and came to a screeching halt in front of the store's automatic double sliding doors. With my car parked in the fire lane, I jumped out, and rushed inside and grabbed my cell phone out my purse and dialed 911.

"911, what's your emergency?" the female dispatcher asked.

"I need the police to come to the Super Food Mart on Rivers Ave. in North Charleston."

"What is the problem, ma'am?"

"Someone is following me and trying to kill me."

"What is your name, ma'am?"

"Laila Roberts. I need you to send someone now."

"Who is trying to kill you?"

"Oh my God, enough with the questions, can you just please just send someone now?"

"Ma'am, in order to help you, I need to ask you these questions. I have police on their way."

"Do you know who the suspects are?"

"No. They were in a black Acura Integra coupe and a white Ford F-150. They chased me in the parking lot of the store, and for the last 10-15 minutes have been following me in the parking lot."

"And you don't know who they are?"

"No, but I can also tell you I didn't let anyone know I was here at the Super Food Mart. They obviously put a GPS tracking device on my car."

"A tracking device? Who would want to put a tracker on your car?"

I agitatedly explained how a couple of people came to my apartment earlier in the day in my best friend Gina's silver Infiniti car to cause trouble. They came to forcibly enter my place to attack me. I reported this to the Mt. Pleasant police in the morning.

"Why are you in North Charleston if you live in Mt. Pleasant?"

"I stopped in the parking lot to make a phone call."

"OK. Who came to your house?"

"My friend Gina's daughter, Caleb McElroy, and Tabatha Baxter."

"And who are they to you?"

"These are my friends."

"Your friends came to your house to assault you?"

"Well, obviously they are not my friends as I thought they were, but yes."

Lurking behind a tall-stacked soda display, I said, "Two of them are coming in the store now. It's the same two in the black Acura."

"You see the suspects in the store?"

"Yes."

"Can you describe what they look like? What are they wearing?"

She radioed to another dispatcher, "Hispanic female, approximately 5', 4", wearing a black hooded sweatshirt; white male, short, husky, approximately 5' 5", wearing blue jeans and a red plaid fleece jacket."

"What color shoes do they have on?"

"I have no idea what color shoes they have on. I did not see their shoes. They are walking toward the back of the store. Hurry! They're going to get away."

"Ma'am, where are you in the store?"

"I'm now near Aisle 12, trying to keep an eye on them."

"The police are pulling up now so I need you to go toward the front of the store."

"OK, I'm walking toward the front now."

"You should see two uniformed patrol officers on the scene."

"I don't see them," I said I as kept an eye on the suspects while also glancing at the entrance for the cops. "OK, I actually see the officers now."

"The officers will take it from here. Good luck with the situation," she said before hanging up.

the chase

The two officers approached me. I stated again what I told to the 911 dispatcher. They said they heard everything over the radio. I gave them the description of the two suspects in the store who were checking out in Lane 7 buying a candy bar and a soda pop. Their purchase was to make it seem like they went into the grocery store to make a purchase as opposed to the real reason. The officers motioned for store security to come over to sit with me while they went to locate and question the young suspects.

I stood there with the young male security officer whom appeared to be in early 20's. He looked and sounded inexperienced. Good thing his job was only to stay with me for a short time until the police completed their investigation. Shortly after, the officers returned unconvinced about the pair following me.

"We spoke to the two suspects," the officer said.

"And?"

"They said they weren't following you, and that they didn't even know you?"

"That's what they're supposed to say!"

49

"They are both high school teenagers. They said they came into the store to buy a couple of candy bars and a soda. In fact, they said you were following them around in the store."

"I followed them because I didn't want them to get away. Once they noticed me watching them, they began walking toward the exit doors on the opposite side of the store."

"Well, if it's any consolation, we are actually going arrest them for unrelated charges. We're going to take them down to the station since they had marijuana on them. It's a small amount so we'll probably just have their parents pick them up from the station. At least you know they won't be around here to follow you home, so that should make you feel a little better."

I was somewhat relieved but did not want to get in my car since I believed a GPS tracker was secretly installed. Instead of going inside, I sat at one of the tables in the full-service deli area and called my cousin Big Red to pick me up. I didn't want to call him at 11:30 at night but also did not want to call any other family members since my friends knew the obvious ones I would call. Big Red lived 35 minutes away and said he'd leave to pick me up once he threw some clothes on.

In the meantime, I sat and talked with the young security officer who was nice enough to keep me company. Forty-five minutes passed and Big Red hadn't arrived. As the security officer and I talked, we both noticed a couple with hooded sweatshirts walk into the store. They glanced over at us, made eye contact with me, abruptly stopped and pivoted toward the Red Box video rental kiosk. These were the same two in the Ford F-150 that tried to block me in.

"Those are the other two who were following me," I discretely said to the security officer.

He glimpsed over at them, and hastily looked back at me. They left the Red Box without a rental, proceeded to walk in the store and took their hoods off their head. Once again, I called 911.

"911, what is your emergency?"

It was déjà vu all over again. The same exasperating scenario repeated itself with the dispatcher asking me a series of annoying questions. I repeatedly asked her to send someone back to the Super Food Mart. In five minutes the same two male officers arrived. They hadn't gotten very far from just leaving, and the two suspects they arrested were in a car with two other officers headed to the station. I was pleased to see them and walked up to them.

"Ms. Roberts, we got a call you needed us to come back."

"Yes, the other two that were following me in the white Ford pickup just came in to the store."

"What did they look like?"

I gave their description and told them that the security officer followed them to the back of the store. They had the customer service manager page the security officer over the store's intercom system. When the security officer returned he gave the location of the suspects. The police officers located the suspects and questioned them just as they did they last two. Identical to the previous pair, they told the officers they didn't know me and were just area high school students who came into the grocery store for a late-night snack. I knew that wasn't the truth but didn't have proof.

It became clear to me Caleb and Landan were behind this and employed Caleb's son's high school friends to follow me. He told me many times of him and Landan recruiting high school students to do various things for them. They both adopted the philosophy from the book "48 Laws of Power" to "keep your hands clean," so they enlisted others to do their dirty work.

"I'm not driving my car or leaving until my cousin arrives. I am not aware of who else is out there waiting for me. I don't know what's going on and I don't feel safe," I said to the officers. "Is there a safe house you can get me to?"

"We don't have any place like that to take you."

"What about a shelter?"

"You'll have to call one of the local shelters or 211 for suggestions," the officer said.

I reiterated I was worried about leaving the store and needed their help. It had already been an hour and my cousin Big Red still hadn't arrived. I was now even more irritated, uneasy, and helpless. My anxiety grew. I became paranoid. I didn't know where to turn. The officers recognized my paranoia and offered to help.

"Ms. Roberts, we need to ask you a couple of questions first."

"OK, no problem."

"These are standard questions and are not meant to offend you."

"OK, that's fine. Ask away."

"Are you under any type of medication?"

"What? No!"

"We have to ask you this, Ms. Roberts."

"Have you taken any type of drugs within the last 24 hours?"

"Gosh no."

"Are you feeling like yourself?"

"Other than the fact that someone is after me, I feel fine. I'm not on drugs or medication, and never did any drugs. I'm very coherent and competent. Someone is just trying to kill me, and I don't feel safe."

"We can't take you to a shelter, but we can take you to the hospital. Would you like us to take you there?"

"Yes, of course, if it's going to help me feel safe."

"We can only take you as a patient to the hospital if you're experiencing paranoia and not feeling like yourself."

I wanted to leave the store and this seemed to be the only way out since Big Red still hadn't arrived. The officers coached me on what to say to meet the hospital's criteria, and I told them exactly what I needed to in order to have them take me.

"Well, in that case, I'm experiencing paranoia and I'm not feeling like myself."

"EMS would have to transport you in the ambulance."

"Even better."

Using police jargon, the officer requested an ambulance. He discussed the hospital's protocol with me and wanted me to know they were taking me to the Crisis Center. Unfamiliar with the Crisis Center, I assumed it was an interchangeable term for the emergency room. He explained the Crisis Center would conduct a psychological evaluation because I said I experienced paranoia. I agreed to everything in order to get to a safe location without anyone knowing my whereabouts.

While waiting for the ambulance, the officers escorted me to my car to move it from the fire lane. Once the ambulance arrived, they helped me through the side door of the ambulance and left me in the hands of two male EMT's. They securely strapped me to the gurney, took my vitals and asked me a series of medical-related questions. They needed to inspect my purse before leaving, for safety reasons, and noticed an 8-inch wooden-handle utility knife.

With blue latex gloves on, the EMT held the knife up and asked, "Why do you have this knife?"

"For protection. I grabbed it out my house. People came there and were after me."

"We'll need to discard this before we can leave for the hospital."

"That's fine, no problem."

the crisis center

I later realized, a section of the emergency room was in fact the psychiatric Crisis Center. I still didn't mind because no one knew where I was and I felt safe. The EMT's wheeled me in to one of the patient rooms. The triage nurse came in to ask the same routine questions, handed me a turquoise hospital gown, and asked me to get undressed from the waist up. She sharply told me she'd be back in a few minutes and locked the door behind her. She was an intimidating thin white brunette. Outside the door, the responding officers briefed her on my account of the events. Their muffled voices barely came through the thick wooden door, and I couldn't make sense of their conversation because the police radio and other conversations cluttered in the background. Nevertheless, I knew they were talking about me.

The room was cold and gloomy. It was not a standard patient room. It didn't have a phone or TV, just a sink, bed, and a no-cell-phone sign. When I noticed the sign, I knew I needed to hide my phone before Nurse Ratchet returned. She'd already taken my purse and other belongings. I only had eight per cent battery life left on my phone and needed to call Big

Red to let him know I was at the hospital. I asked him to be on standby in case I needed him to pick me up in a couple of hours. I quickly called my 13-year-old son Zion to let him know what was going on. He already knew my friends had come to the house earlier. I did not have much time so I needed him to pay close attention as I quickly explained my friends were now trying to kill me. I remembered a few times one of Caleb's relatives surprisingly mentioned my life insurance policy, and that's what they were after. Zion was half asleep and I could tell he wasn't attentively listening since it was one o'clock in the morning.

"Zion?" I shouted.

"Huh?"

"Wake up! I need you to pay attention."

"OK"

"I'm at the emergency room and as soon as I leave in a couple hours, I'm coming to pick you up. Have your clothes ready."

"Why?"

"We are going to have to leave the area for a little while because people are trying to kill me."

He was already aware Gina's daughter along with Tabatha and Caleb came to my house earlier. Much of this surprised him because Gina's daughters were his god-sisters and they all grew up together. Gina's selfishness and consistent quest for someone else's man made her irrational. She did not think about the consequences of her indiscretions nor the effect it might have on our children's relationship. She simply didn't think about the possible overall outcome. She was confident of not getting caught because she assumed her relationship with Caleb would remain hush-hush, as did with her 10-year affair with a married man.

Nevertheless, I told Zion not to trust any of my friends and to stay away from them in case they came by trying to trick him into leaving with them or letting them in the house. He was still half sleep but understood my once-trusted friends were now evil enemies. I assured him I'd pick him up as soon as I left the hospital and demanded he stay in the house.

He was reluctant to go along with the plan to leave town. He had just entered his teenage years, had many friends, and did not want to relocate once again. In the last 11 years this would have been his third school, and relocating is an adjustment for any kid. He was doing well and I planned to keep him in his private Mt. Pleasant school, which was rated one of the top schools in the Charleston area. As a parent, it was dreadful to drag my son though this nonsense. Further, it was embarrassing to tell him that the people I once loved and trusted as family turned on me. The situation was a nightmare.

I heard the door to my room unlock and the nurse walked in.

"Cell phones are not allowed," she shouted. "You need to turn off your phone and give it to me to lock up. You can have back after you're discharged."

"I just need to call my cousin to come to the hospital," I pleaded.

"Laila, make your call. I'll be back in a few minutes. When I come back, I'll need your phone and a urine sample."

I called my grandmother and uncle as well as my 27-year-old cousin Olivia to let them know what was going on and my whereabouts. I referred to Olivia and her older sister, Navia, as my little sisters. She was in shock of what was going on because she was well acquainted with Gina through me and couldn't believe Gina nor Tabatha would turn on me. She didn't know their true character as I did. I couldn't talk long because my phone was dying. I'll told them I'd call back later on.

Lying there cold on my hospital bed with a thin blanket, I tried to finish piecing this nonsense together. "How did they have an opportunity to put a GPS tracker on my car?" I asked myself. I could not wrap my brain around what was happening. It seemed like a very bad dream. I thought back to the recent weeks when my car was out of my sight, which wasn't often. I parked it in my garage at home and in the parking lot at my job — and once at the local repair shop. That's when the dots connected. The pieces of the puzzle fit nicely. Caleb knew I was scheduled to take my car to the auto shop near his house a few days prior to my friends coming to my house. I remembered I sent him a text asking him for a ride home from the shop since it was near his house and I was less than three miles from him. A friend of the family, Ryan, who I affectionately called Butter Kup because of his milky skin, also knew I was going to the repair shop because he referred me to the shop mechanic.

He called the shop's owner to schedule the service appointment for me and worked out a sweet deal. I wasn't certain but felt one of them arranged to have the tracker placed on my car even though, as with those following me at the grocery store, I didn't have evidence. I also recalled the mechanic driving around the corner with my car once he took it off the lift and having me wait two hours for a simple repair. I assumed he took it for a test drive but now believe he drove to meet Caleb or Butter Kup with the device.

Too add to the theory, Butter Kup was at the house around that same time and suggested I download a new user-friendly GPS app to my smartphone. He raved about the features of this new cool app and said it would allow us both to virtually see and time each other while we were driving. We both drove a lot for our jobs and regularly talked to each other while driving. He said while we talked we could time each other and see each other's location while getting more accurate directions to our destinations than the standard GPS. It sounded compelling and sophisticated so I downloaded the app. He and I never used the app once I installed it nor did he mention it again. Ironically, I almost deleted it from my phone to create additional data storage space on my phone. One of the two theories occurred if not both. While waiting for the nurse to return, I Googled the GPS app and right away the caption on the app's website professed the app to be the world's most sophisticated surveillance software. I read through the website in amazement. The software, which gave each user's real-time location, had been used by the government for surveillance and intelligence. I almost dropped my phone in disbelief as if coal was burning in the palm of my hand. I couldn't believe Butter Kup was in on this too. I wanted to throw the phone against the wall in anger but I needed it. Instead I deleted the app and turned off the location services from my phone's privacy settings.

I had enough compelling evidence to call the police. As with the last two earlier 911 calls, I endured the frustration of answering the same monotonous questions. My battery was dying. I did not have much time to be on the phone. I spoke softly and fast and explained Caleb McElroy or Ryan Gause put a tracker on my phone, tracked me at the Super Food Mart on Rivers Ave. in North Charleston, and they were trying to kill me. The operator pinpointed my location and asked why I called from Charleston if I lived in Mt. Pleasant, and why I was calling from Southern Coastal Hospital.

While on the phone with the cops, the nurse busted in the room, reached her hand to me and demanded my cell phone. When I told her I needed

61

to make another call, she snatched the phone out from my fingers.

"I need your phone now!" the nurse shouted. "No more calls."

She rushed to the nurse's station and picked up the desk phone to continue speaking to the caller she had placed on hold. Surprisingly, she was talking to the caller about me.

"OK, I have her phone," she said. "The calls she made?"

"Who the hell is she talking to?" I asked myself.

"She called 911, Big Red, Zion, Grandma, Olivia, and it looks like she called Big Red again and 911 three times."

"Who are you talking to?" I asked her.

"Go back into your room, Laila" she screamed. "I am on the phone with the police. They called the hospital since you called them. You need to go back into your room."

This woman, I thought, was truly acting like Nurse Ratchet. I must have watched too my reruns of her role in "One Flew Over the Cuckoo's Nest."

When she returned to the room, she handed me my phone and commanded I turn the power off. She needed to secure my phone and restrict my calls. There was no reasoning with this woman. She was firm and curt, and she didn't bother to ask me any questions or give me an opportunity to tell her what was going on. I tried to interject to explain I called the cops because I discovered someone downloaded a GPS tracker app on my phone.

"You didn't say anything about an app on your phone earlier, you said someone put a tracker on your car."

"I just remembered the app a few minutes ago."

"No more calls, Laila. Please go into the bathroom and give me a urine sample."

She was behaving like a bitch and I wanted to call her exactly that but felt she might lash back since she was so feisty. I didn't want any trouble and didn't want her to continue giving me a hard time. I had a lot on my mind and was already dealing with today's ordeal. The discovery of the GPS tracking app on my phone and her badgering contributed to my excruciating headache. Further, I could not think clearly so much that each time I went into the communal bathroom with the specimen cup, I forgot to give her a urine sample. She thought I did it on purpose and became upset. After the third time of going to the bathroom and forgetting, she was even more frustrated and impatient.

"Laila, I really need the specimen. You will not be able to meet with the intake counselor for the evaluation until we receive a urine sample. Here's a large cup of water, please drink it. If you forget this time, I'm going to have to put a catheter in you."

"Bitch," I mumbled under my breath.

To comply and get her off my back, I forcibly gulped down four cups of water.

the standoff

I was reassigned to another dark, gloomy cold room without a door. Not only that, it also didn't have a sink, phone, bathroom, or light switch. From the doorway opening was a long, dark, quiet hallway with nine other door-less rooms and a well-lit nurse's station at the corridor's far left corner. Nurses were in the middle of changing work shifts and the nurse assigned to me was waiting for the Crisis Center's social worker to facilitate my evaluation. Just as with Nurse Ratchet, this nurse was impatient and annoyed with me each time I asked questions.

The raspy voice of a middle-aged woman echoed throughout the halls. I scooted to the edge of my bed to eavesdrop to find out what the commotion was about. The patient was shouting obscenities at the nurse and demanded the nurse move away from her because the devil was behind her. I peeked from the doorway to get a glance but could not see the woman and nurse. However, I saw a tall man pacing back and forth down the corridor with this hands behind his back while another nurse urged him to return to his room.

Shortly after that, my nurse walked in the room.

"Laila Roberts?"

"Yes"

"My name is Sylvia. I am one of the nurses and am going to prepare you to meet with the clinical social worker who is going to conduct your psychological evaluation."

"OK, great."

"We're going into the conference room next door. I need to check your wristband for your name and date of birth," she said.

We walked down the dark hall and sat at a small round table in the tight conference room which apparently was converted from a small patient room.

"Before we begin, I need to make a phone call to my son," I said. "I need my cell phone back."

"Security has your phone locked up, but you can you the nurses' cordless phone."

She handed me an outdated cordless phone with a long silver antenna. I called Zion to update him on the details and to let him know I was still at the hospital. After each question I asked him, I could hear the swift motion of the phone going back and forth as if someone else had control of the phone and held it to his ear. I purposely asked Zion subsequent questions and carefully listened for the back-and-forth whisk sound again while the phone went from ear to ear.

"Is someone there with you Zion?"

"No," he said in a slurred and slowed response.

I became worried about his safety. I asked him to hand the phone to my Uncle George who was in Charleston visiting from Philadelphia. Alarmingly, the same air-whisked sound of the phone going back and forth occurred many times during my call with Uncle George. He asked if I was OK, if I was taking my medication, if I was still hearing voices, and he insisted I come to the Grandma's.

"Hearing voices? Medication? What are you talking about?" I confusedly probed.

He repeated the same thing. I remembered Gina said the same to me on the phone during our shouting match two days ago. "What the hell is going on?" I wondered. Clearly, something was happening at my grandmother's house, and it could also be linked to Gina since it's a mirror of what she said just a couple days ago.

After my verbal fight with her the other day, she sent me a text which read, "It is too bad you phucked up our 20-year friendship. I know how crazy you are and you hear voices in your head."

This became worse than a nightmare. It was surreal that I experienced this. I also knew the text was driven or written by Caleb. He was always quick to grab someone else's phone to send or respond to a text. These were his words and things he said to me in the past to annoy me.

It was obvious he or someone connected to him was at my grandmother's house with Uncle George, planted the same crazy-hearing-voices seeds about me, and forced Uncle George to say this to me. It wasn't anything he or Gina had ever said to me before. It seemed orchestrated and rehearsed. Intuitively, I knew something was wrong and someone was holding them against their will. Uncle George continued to insist I come to the house and kept asking in a panicky voice about my whereabouts. To keep him calm, I told him to just pray and that I was in a secure location. I didn't disclose my location because I did not want anyone there to know.

He repeated everything I said for whomever to know what I said. I told him I was calling for help and would send someone. When he said, "OK," it confirmed that intruders where there holding them hostage. Before the phone hung up, I heard Uncle George moan and say, "Oh no, what are you doing?" The nurse was still in the room with me and heard this unfold because the phone's speaker was on. She had a concerned and terrified look on her face which spoke volumes.

"You heard that?" I asked her.

She nodded yes and said, "You need to call the police. Something is terribly wrong."

Using the nurse's cordless phone, I called the

police once again. This time instead of dialing 911, I called directory assistance for the non-emergency number for the Charleston police station to avoid the redundant questions.

"Lockwood Station, Officer Towanski."

"Hi, I need the police to go to 74 North Lenox Ave. There's a hostage-situation there."

"A hostage situation? Who is being held hostage?"

"My son, uncle and grandmother at 74 N. Lenox Avenue in Charleston."

"Who is holding them hostage?"

"I'm not sure who or how many, but someone is there, possibly with guns."

"Are you at the house now?"

"No, I'm at the hospital, but need you to send someone to the house now."

"Ok, we're sending a car now."

The clinical social worker came in the conference room and the nurse left with the cordless phone. The social worker was soft-spoken with a slow and therapeutic voice. She advised me she was there to conduct my evaluation and it wasn't going to take long. As with the other intakes, she asked a series of questions to gauge my mental health. I remained focused on her questions despite being distracted by the hostage situation at my grandmother's house and the safety of my family.

She calmly advised me her questions were routine but needed to be asked in order to rule out any mental disorders and arrive at a hypothesis about my health and stability. Her objective was also to determine if I was a candidate for admission in the hospital. I understood the customary questions since I been through it twice already with the police and Crisis Center intake. I was not opposed since I was of sound mind and had requested to come to the Crisis Center for personal safety.

She inquired about my work and family background, and asked me describe a typical day. She wanted to know about my emotions, recent stress, current life problems and any possible thoughts of injuring myself or others. She gently reminded me these questions were not geared to offend me and proceeded to ask her standardized evaluation questions. Her demeanor was very kind, soft, and welcoming. She showed great listening skills, great eye contact, asked genuine follow-up questions and used many nonverbal gestures to show she was listening. Just as much, she seemed genuine, compassionate, and nonjudgmental. These characteristics helped to develop trust, credibility, and comfort which also helped me open up about my personal life.

With her eyes glued to mine, we continued to talk for another 45 minutes. I cooperated with the assessment and when finished, she asked me if I wanted to add anything before a recommendation was made. I was relieved to let her know what occurred earlier in the day but used caution in my delivery because I knew everything was under scrutiny. Calmly, I spoke to her in a tone of professionalism and conviction. I explained with persuasion I am a chemist in the pharmacy industry and a visiting lecturer at the local medical college. I travel the world speaking at various conferences to medical and pharmaceutical professionals. Further, I am well-accomplished with several degrees and have a Ph.D. in biomedical chemistry.

"I am very competent, coherent, and of sound mind," I proclaimed.

She nodded in agreement.

"Today was one of the most unusual days of my life."

I told her about my earlier phone conversation with my friend Tabatha. She and I had two conversations around 6 a.m. and again at 8:30, which was not unusual. But, I said, her demeanor and tone during the second phone call were very different from the first. We spoke about the conflict and verbal shouting match Gina and I had two days earlier on Christmas Eve. She knew I was aware Gina was sleeping with Caleb behind my back and knew how I found out. She went on to say Caleb was a dangerous person. During our call, Tabatha asked me to pay close attention to the clues she indirectly gave as she spoke in a rational and compassionate tone.

Tabatha said, "Listen, you're very smart and can put things together. You need to listen to what I'm saying and read between the lines."

"Go on," I said.

"Caleb is a very dangerous man with bad intentions. He's very manipulative with an evil spirit. He is not a good person and you should have never let him in your life. I hate you ever met him."

"Go on," the social worker insisted.

"She said he came into your life during a vulnerable moment in your life, right after your cousin's death. His timing in your life was no coincidence. You have to be very careful of who you let in your life."

She recalled conversations I shared with her about him.

"Remember you told me he created a horrible lie about someone and spread it as a rumor around town to embarrass the person?"

"Yeah?"

"Well, indirectly he was telling you his plan to publicly embarrass you by spreading a rumor about you. He also planned to have you lured to a familiar place, have your clothes stripped off you, have you beaten naked while videotaping it to post on Facebook.

He was planning to humiliate you."

"What?"

"Yeah, I don't think he knows how much he hurt you that caused you to react the way you did when you found out he was messing around with the younger girl he's often around at his cousin's house. He's planning to get even with you, and it isn't good — hell, it's not even. He is planning to go way too far. I have always told you, you met your match with him."

"Way too far?"

Suddenly, I had a realization that explained my tormenters' determination to get rid of me. It was so simple, I couldn't believe I'd not thought of it before. The motive was money. And it came in the form of my life insurance policy entrusted to Gina.

I explained this to the social worker along with my friends' plot to kill me for my half-million life insurance policy. I couldn't believe I was telling this story because it sounded crazy, ridiculous and psychotic. I was embarrassed to share the story because of how flaky, unbelievable, and imaginary it sounded.

Three months prior while at Charleston's Waterfront Park for dinner on the stationary boat, Caleb and Landan overheard Gina was named the executor and trustee of my Will. Initially they plotted against me as the request of Brent, but once they heard of my fortune and assets their conspiracy thickened since much more was at stake. Gina was like a sister to me and although I had other family and sisters, she was someone I deeply trusted and felt comfortable designating her as the executor and trustee to manage the funds for my minor son in the event something ever happened to me. Over the last two years, I silently observed her manage the finances of her ailing grandparents. I admired her dedication and management of their health and finances, and felt she could do the same for Zion's finances and college expenses.

Caleb and Landan saw an opportunity. As the adage goes "for the love of money is root of all evil." Even though Caleb and Gina were fooling around he subsequently forged a closer relationship with her that extended beyond just sex in effort to get her emotionally attached to him. The death benefits were over a half a million dollars and the real estate portfolio of my estate.

He also knew Gina was very insecure with herself and only dated unavailable men because those were the only men she was able to get. She was a 5-foot average- looking shallow woman who masked her insecurities with short skirts or tight leggings, scissor-cut boob-revealing shirts and bright red lip gloss to gain the attention of men who otherwise would not have noticed her. She prided herself in having fun with someone else's husband, and enjoyed the thrill of designing schemes to help them sneak with her. Over 15 years ago she suffered a terrible breakup and feared repeated heartache so she only involved herself with unavailable men to remain emotionally disconnected.

She championed the role of the other woman. Even though she was currently involved in a 10-year affair with a married man and seeing a few others on the side, Caleb's manipulative charm mesmerized her and chiseled through the walls of hard heart. She became in awe with him and called him her "Black Obama," Tabatha said, referring to his darker skin tone. Gina couldn't believe he was interested in her. In our 20 years of friendship, I rarely seen or heard a man make any serious advancements toward her. If they did, they were only interested in a good time because they knew she was a lot of fun and could keep a secret.

My point in telling this to the social worker was to bring her to my next point, which was the second phone call with Tabatha that morning. The second call started with normal small talk. She was preparing to go to Macy's at Northwood Mall in Charleston by herself, and said she would have invited me if I didn't hate going to the mall with people. It wasn't uncommon for people not to invite me because they knew how much I despised going shopping at malls with people. I preferred to get in and get out.

I heard her get in her car but also heard another door shut. Once she was in her car, her conversation and tone completely changed. She shifted from shopping-talk to scattered comments related to Gina and Caleb, and bits and pieces about things I solely said and texted to Caleb. Majority of the texts were about me demeaning Gina in regards to her using my health insurance for an abortion, past sexually transmitted diseases, false front teeth, and the number of men she's currently sleeping with. During her conversation, Tabatha paused many times and in mid-sentence she'd switch to something we already discussed in the first phone call. Her scattered conversation, irrational tone and interim pauses heightened my radar. It wasn't hard to differentiate the tone of two conversations and she was making points to appease someone else who was in the car with her.

Tabatha, who also lacks self-confidence, had a need for belonging and association, and fell into Landan's quest to form a cult-like following of weak people. She has a strong desire to have a sense of attachment to a cause or a person to validate her existence. She forms an allegiance to create the perception of belonging because the connection makes her feel significant, relevant, and better about herself regardless of the unhealthy attachment. Sadly, she often compromises her integrity and values as she struggles to prove herself and her loyalty to others. Her logic of loyalty is distorted by immaturity, persuasion and simple reasoning – and bad influence. Ironically, she has a good heart but out of desperation has been corrupted by affiliation with Gina and Landan. Gina also convinced her it acceptable to deal with unavailable men when it was something Tabatha was firmly against. I always told her stop listening to Gina's advice nor follow in her footsteps because bad company corrupts good character.

While on the phone with me, Tabatha made indirect references to me when referring to someone else. Much of her conversation did not make any sense. She made pointless and redundant comments which caused further suspicion largely because this was erratic, disturbing and significantly different than earlier. Tabatha continued to repeat herself with frequent interval pauses while she tried to intentionally keep me on the phone while she, Gina's daughter and Caleb drove to my house. They planned to enter my house with the key Caleb secretly made a copy of, catch me off guard, and carry out their plans to violently attack me.

"She knew of my personal text messages to Caleb because she was reading them from his phone since he was in the car," I said to the social worker. "It makes sense now why she kept pausing and jumping around in the conversation because she was pausing to read the texts and indirectly mentioning them."

This wasn't surprising because Tabatha is a very messy person and can always be found in the midst of trouble or gossip. Although I was a little taken back by her deceit, I was not surprised. After all, her allegiance was to Gina. They were friends first, and I met Tabatha through Gina. Albeit juvenile, this was Tabatha's formula for loyalty. Remaining neutral was in opposition of her need to feel connected to someone or a cause. If she remained neutral, it would make her feel she does not a place and the lack of attachment would further damage her low self-esteem.

The social worker looked at me in amazement. I explained my family was being held hostage, and the nurse and I heard my uncle moaning on the phone say,

"Oh no! What are you doing?" The look on her face was intense.

She said, "After this evaluation, my assessment is that you are not psychotic or suffering from paranoia, and your story is very real."

"Thank you."

"I'm very sorry you are going through this. You are not a candidate for admission, however, I am going to recommend you stay here in the Crisis Center for the time you need in order for you to get help."

I felt a huge sense of relief, as she gave me the forms and instructions to voluntarily admit myself to the unit.

"I'll get your cell phone from security to allow you to jot down a few numbers to make emergency calls from the nurse's phone. I'll need to lock your phone back up since personal phones are not allowed on the floor."

no visitors allowed

The place I came to feel safe became the very place I feared. Under no circumstances was anyone to know I was a patient on the fifth floor of the hospital. To safeguard my identity, I signed in under an alias. After hearing the painful moan of my uncle at the mercy of my assailants invading my grandmother's house, disclosing my location to family was not an option. People who once professed to be my friends had overtaken my family in bloody thirst for my life. For hours they waited at my grandmother's for my call to learn my whereabouts. Armed with weapons and intimidation, the intruders made countless threats to my uncle, ultimately forcing him to try to convince me it was safe to return home. Their whispered demands echoed in the background while they snatched the phone from ear to ear. I detected their voices in the background as they listened to my plea.

"Just pray, Uncle George, everything's going to be OK. I'm going to send for help."

"I'm praying, I'm praying. Are you OK?"

"Yes, I'm OK."

"Where are you?"

"I'm in a secure location?"

"You're in a secure location?"

"Yes."

"Just come to the house."

"Why?"

"Just come to the house, Laila."

"OK, I'll be there."

"You're on your way now?"

"Yes."

Going to the house wasn't part of the plan. I needed my uncle to think I was on my way. But by repeating everything I said he confirmed the assailants were still in the house. Running scared through the wilderness of my own mind, strategies for survival and heroism played over and over. Freeing my family from the horrific nightmare was my primary focus. I was limited from calling the police since I called so many times from the Crisis Center. Doing so again meant revocation of my phone privileges.

I had to think smart. Unsure of how to sneak the opportunity to call to the authorities, I paced back and forth down the hall. To beat their implemented phone-bully system, I called a political power player to call the cops for me. Maynard was the Deputy Mayor and a longtime family friend whom I'd known since I was a child. He was an older, vibrant man originally from Alabama with a rich Southern accent. The town members considered him a maverick because he was a force to be reckoned with. Over the years we'd lost touch, but no matter how long the time lapse he was sure to jump in the fire. First, I needed his number.

"Directory assistance, what city and state, please?"

"Charleston, South Carolina"

"Person's name?"

"Maynard Gibson"

"I have a Maynard Gibson on Phillips Avenue."

"Yes, that's it."

"Please hold for the listing."

It didn't take long for Maynard to answer the phone in his deep voice. It was difficult to hear with all the commotion and kids in the background. The grandkids were just leaving following their traditional Friday after Christmas at Grandpa's. Maynard and I hadn't spoken in years, but right away he was happy to hear my voice.

"Hey, Laila, so good to hear your voice. How are you my dear?"

"I'm good, Mr. Gibson. How are you?"

"Well, the old man's hanging in there, I must say."

"Mr. Gibson, I called because I need you to do me a huge favor."

"I sure will try."

"I hate to even ask, but I made several calls earlier today and haven't gotten any results."

"What's going on?"

"I'm at Southern Coastal Hospital. My grandmother, uncle and son are being held hostage at my grandmother's house. I called the local police, but when they went to the house they didn't go inside to inspect to make sure no one was keeping them against their will. My uncle told the police they're OK, but he was forced to lie."

"Good Lord! What in the world?"

"Yes, this is horrible so I need you to call someone to go over there. And make sure they go inside."

"Oh my goodness, I just can't believe this. What I'll do is call the sergeant and have him send an unmarked car."

"Ok, great, but make sure they don't send Officer Howard."

"What's going on with Officer Howard?"

"He's a corrupt officer and working with the intruders. Each time I called the cops, Howard was the responding officer and purposely didn't go inside to check the house. He and LJ are in on this together."

"LJ too? What in the heck is wrong with LJ?"

"Yes, so I was hoping you would call one of your colleagues and the FBI."

"OK."

"But you can't call their main number because they've been intercepting my calls from this line."

"Heavens."

"Soon as you're done, call me back on this line. You're the only person I gave this number to."

"OK, give me a few minutes, let me make a couple calls, and I'll give you a call back."

I anxiously awaited his call while sitting near the patient-shared phone bolted to the wall in front on the nurse's station. Phones weren't allowed in the rooms to ensure the patients' tranquility and relaxation, but it's the very thing that would drive a person insane. Mr. Gibson was always known for being long-winded and holding extremely long phone conversations. For this reason, he needed more than a few minutes. Thirty minutes passed and still no callback. I needed to know how he made out.

"Hello?"

"Hey, Mr. Gibson. How'd you make out?"

"Well, I called the FBI and they said it's out of their jurisdiction. You'll need to call the local police since it's their jurisdiction, but when I called the local police they said they've been out to your grandmother's many times and there isn't an issue. Are you OK?"

"Oh goodness, Mr. Gibson, don't tell me they got to you too."

"I don't know what's going on here and who has the ability to intercept phone towers, but I am not with any conspiracy-shit. Who is intercepting phone lines?"

"Did someone intercept your call?"

"They sure did."

"OK, Mr. Gibson. I don't know what to say. I'm going to have to find help another way."

The mentioning of phone and tower interception reminded me of the similar incident that happened while I was in the Crisis Center. I made several calls to the police and then to the mayor's office when the issue of the police inadequately responding to the hostage situation was unresolved. When I dialed the mayor's office, the phone call was intercepted and rerouted to someone working with the assailants. The person who answered sounded like a white older man, probably in his late 40's or early 50's with a deep stern voice.

After explaining to the man supposedly at the

Mayor's office what was going on at my grandmother's, he said, "So you're telling me there's a hostage situation?"

"Yes, and the local police are not going inside to inspect the house to make sure my family is OK. I even pleaded for help on my Facebook page."

"Your family is being held hostage?"

"Yes, they are."

"Aren't you calling from Southern Coastal Hospital?"

"Yes, I'm here. I came here for safety."

"Well, my suggestion for you is to stay away from windows, sharp objects and stay inside. Otherwise you'll find yourself in a hostage situation too."

"What in the world? Are you serious?"

"Yes, I'm very serious. You'll be held captive next."

With this phone call and the one with Mr. Gibson, it was shocking that someone intercepted my phone calls. In both cases, I didn't engage further because it was clear someone on the outside knew where I was and had the ability to remotely access and control the calls from the hospital phone. I stood in the cold hospital corridor, paralyzed by disbelief, wanting to bang my head against the wall. This seemed like a terror scene in an Alfred Hitchcock film playing the realities of my life. It was a mystery I couldn't solve.

Caleb mentioned many times Landan had high-level connections within the Charleston police department and knew someone with network telecommunications expertise. It became clear who other than just Landan had connections inside the hospital, network telecommunication experts, and a hand in this nightmare. Landan had connections and influence on the people in his cult-like following. I never realized so many people were weak and able to be controlled as if they don't have a brain to think for themselves. It was pathetic.

Still trying to piece the puzzle together, I sat bundled with a thin blanket in the green leather recliner in the hallway in front of the nurse's station. The station was secured with glass walls and two locked doors, centered in the middle of the unit with patient rooms on one side, and a recreation and dining hall on the other. Deep in thought, I tuned out the patients talking in the nearby dining hall and became oblivious to everything around me until the doorbell rang. This unit was completely secure with a 24-hour lockdown and four cameras outside the thick metal door. Staff and hospital personnel could gain entrance only with an employee swipe key-card. Those without a card had to ring the doorbell to gain entry. Each time the bell rang, I practically jumped out of my chair, became paranoid, and reminded the nursing staff no one was to know I was here. However, people somehow discovered my whereabouts and called to speak to me. All morning and afternoon, people kept ringing the bell, asking for me.

"Laila, someone is here to see you."

"No! No one is supposed to know I'm here. I don't want to see any one."

"I know you said that, but it's your cousin Sharon."

"What? I don't have a cousin name Sharon."

"Are you sure? She said she's your cousin, and she seems very concerned about you."

The nurse handed me a small piece of paper with Sharon's full name and number on it. I recognized the last name as a family relation through marriage.

"Laila, maybe you should see your cousin. It might help you and maybe it'll make you feel safe."

"She is not my cousin! I don't know her nor have a relationship with her. Why is she here? She may be a very distant relative through marriage but I personally don't know her."

"So you don't want to see her?"

"Absolutely not. She doesn't know me and certainly not well enough to visit me. Make her leave. I don't want to see her. I don't want to see anyone."

It wasn't long before someone else rang the extremely loud doorbell. The long, annoying buzzer was enough to frighten anyone. Each time it rang, I was startled and could barely breathe. I felt like I needed to hyperventilate in a brown paper bag. Quickly, I jumped out of the hallway recliner, ran to the nurse's station window to watch the camera monitors to see who was outside the locked door. For the tenth time, I reminded the nursing staff to say I wasn't there should anyone ask for me.

"Laila, it's for you. You have another visitor."

"Why are you even telling me when I already said I don't want any visitors?"

"But it's your uncle."

"I don't want to see anyone."

"I think you should see your uncle."

"No, I don't want to him either. They sent him up here."

"They who?"

"My friends who are after me."

"Laila, no one is after you."

"Yes, they are."

"Well, they're not going to get you in here. This is a very safe and secure place. No one will harm you in here, so allow him to come in."

"My uncle isn't even from here and doesn't know his way around so they had to bring him up here. Make him leave."

Desperate to capture me, my friends threatened Uncle George, made him come to force me to leave while the hired attackers waited outside to snatch and force me into their parked white delivery van, waiting to whisk me away.

No sooner had I sat down with a sigh of relief, the doorbell rang again. Throughout the day several more family members and friends came and left messages. Infuriation grew with each visit. My tormenters were determined to get me out the hospital and used people close to me to help them.

The half a million dollar life insurance policy ended in six days and they were running out of time. They planned to catch or murder me by any means necessary.

increased suspicions

Suspicion and distrust lurked in the shadows of the hospital. I was cautious of just about everyone I encountered. I quickly developed an armored exterior and kept my distance from all around me. The after-effects of Gina's betrayal and the double-crossing by my other friends made me question the motives of everyone. Even those with genuine intentions were shunned with resistance and withdrawal. My assailants with ill intentions remained in hot pursuit of my life. Because of that, I kept one eye glued to all comings and goings. I scrutinized the behavior and movement of the people already on the unit and any who entered subsequently. Catnaps during the day and coffee at night enabled me to stay awake throughout the evening. I became the modern-day watch commander of the fifth floor.

The patients slept in their rooms, undisturbed by the loud ticking of the clock on the wall. The staff quietly peeking and tip-toeing in the rooms every 15 minutes didn't seem to interrupt them much, but it annoyed the hell out of me. My room was three doors down and across from the glassed-in nurse's station. The station had locked doors on each side as the nurses worked through the night with their backs facing my room. The 5th floor rooms overlooked Victorian-style homes decorated with a blanket of snow from the recent storm. Icy air seeped through the large drape-less corner windows, adding a shivering chill to the cloud of darkness on top of the cold linoleum floors. Bare beige walls added neither warmth nor charm to the place. What's more, the twin beds separated by a narrow wooden dresser made it look like a Medieval convent. A cross hanging on the wall over the dresser was the only thing missing.

Alone in my room, the silence disturbed me. I walked near the nurse's station and forced myself to stay awake in the green leather recliner. A dim light from their workspace added a glow to the dark hallway. Crossword puzzles, Word Find searches and Sudoku kept my mind occupied as my eyes tried to escape to the land of dreams. I spruced up in the chair to shake off the urge to nod off. I needed to stay awake to monitor the unit for self-protection. I didn't know who was going to sneak on the floor looking for me. Every couple of hours, a respite staff worker came to relieve the nurses for their dinner or cigarette break. The slam of the solid metal door startled me each time.

After two days on the unit, it was my turn to meet with the counseling treatment team that consisted of a social worker, a nurse and a clinical psychiatrist. We met in the morning in a small conference room which also was the library with only 11 books. As I walked into the room in my baggy light blue patient scrubs and patient socks, the shrink pointed to the chair for me to sit down.

"Good morning, Laila. Please have a seat," he said in a heavy Indian accent. "How are you this morning?"

"I'm well. Thanks for asking."

"That's good, Laila. Are you feeling better?"

"I'm feeling fine. Nothing's wrong with me."

"I understand, but do you feel better than you did when you first came here."

"I guess so. However, I still feel unsafe."

"You feel unsafe here?"

"Yes, I do."

"Now why is that?"

"Because my friends who are trying to kill me know I'm in the hospital and are making plans to get to me while here."

"Who is trying to kill you?"

"Actual friends of mine, Caleb McElroy, Landan Jeffries and Brent Sayers."

"Why are your friends trying to kill you?"

"Former friends, but for my half million dollar life insurance policy."

"What interest do they have in your insurance policy?"

"Caleb and Landan both overheard my girlfriend Regina was the Executor and Trustee of my Last Will and Testament. If anything were to happen to me, the half-million dollar lump-sum payment would be issued to her to manage the trust for my son."

"Hmmm, I see."

"Yes, big mistake on my part. Regina and I were very good friends, and I felt comfortable leaving her with that responsibility. I'd known her for 20 years, and was confident I could trust her. Caleb and Landan overheard this and came up with a bright idea. They orchestrated a plan for Caleb to fake a relationship and strong attraction to Gina. They had already been sleeping around behind my back for the past several months but once they found out about the policy, he got closer to her, making her think he was really into her. He's very deceptive and charming. He told her all the right things, everything she wanted to hear — how he wished he'd met her first, that she's more understanding than me and he really enjoyed being with her. Until then, he would sneak over to her house in the mornings before she went to work, or later in the evenings when her lover left to go home to his wife."

"Hmmmm"

"Caleb started spending more time with her, including overnights to make her feel he was really into her and wanted to exclusively be with her. Her married lover was never able to spend overnights with her throughout their 10-year affair, so having that warm, attractive man next to her made her feel wanted and special. She never had anyone so attracted to her, besides; it's been close to 20 years since she's had a man of her own. To continue his deceptive plan, he snuck off to Cape Cod with her for a romantic weekend getaway. Weakened with no boundaries, coupled with his manipulation and charm, she fell for it just as I did. It was all part of his demonic scheme to get closer to her, cause conflict between two trusted friends, and cash in."

"That's pretty compelling, Laila."

"Well, it's pretty true. I never would have imagined this being a part of my life, nor would I have imagined my best friend of 20 years betraying me. I would have expected this from Tabatha but not Gina. My tormenters came to my house two days ago to attack me, but I'd left the house just before they arrived. They were dressed in hooded sweatshirts, leather gloves, and in Gina's silver 4-door car with dark tinted windows. Even through the dark windows, her daughter and I made direct eye contact as she drove down my secluded street in my affluent Mt. Pleasant neighborhood. They had no business on my side of town, 40 miles away from their village of mostly trailer parks. Being in my town made them stick out like a fish out of water. They just did not belong or fit in. Both surprised to notice the other, we drove by like two ships passing in the night. She accelerated and raced down the sloped hill while Caleb instructed her to turn left toward the Interstate to head east of Charleston."

"Go on," the shrink said.

"They wanted me to think her daughter was coming to my house with her uncle, father and their friends. Tabatha mentioned her uncle was getting involved after Gina and I had the verbal fight, but that wasn't entirely true. It was Landan's idea to have Tabatha lie to distract me. She's weak, goes along with anything he suggests, and so desperate for acceptance that she doesn't realize she's being manipulated. They also knew Gina's weaknesses. She likes to make her lover feel she's in his corner, on his team and proves her part as the sideline chick. Their goal was to get me and Gina feuding while Caleb coached her on what to say to me. He and Landan created a fight between Gina and me to divert my attention from them and their plan. Their street philosophy had always been to attack the target when beefing with someone else, and both figured I'd think it was Gina's baby daddy and uncle initiating the turmoil. However, someone secretly tipped me off to their plan."

"Interesting."

"Once I heard they were after my life insurance

policy, I quickly modified my will to terminate Gina as the executor and trustee, and emailed a revised copy to my aunt in East Orange, New Jersey, and another copy to local friend who I later discovered was working with them as well. I sent Gina and Tabatha an email and a text advising them of the change. Gina didn't respond, but Tabatha replied, 'I really hate this. I really do.' She's so full of it. I just said to myself, 'Yeah, I bet you do' and didn't bother replying. Her cut was $25,000 for being the spy and posing as a friend. She mentioned quite a bit that she was expecting $25,000 but I had no idea it was blood money for my life."

"Wow, that's a pretty epic story."

"Tell me about it. They say the love of money is the root of all evil."

"Yeah. That's good you changed your will."

"I know."

"But if you changed the policy, shouldn't you feel better now?"

"No, because they're still after me. They are planning to submit Tabatha and Gina's copy as the binding version. I'm going to need to contact an estate lawyer to modify it again, and have them secure the binding copy and manage my estate."

"That's a really good idea."

"Yeah, I'll take care of that as soon as I get out of

here. Gina, Tabatha and Caleb also have all been in touch with my family to pretend they're concerned about me and my mental stability. It was a pretty clever plan. This was just one more diversion tactic so no one would believe me when I said they were actually the ones after me. They even planted the idea in my family's head that I'm hearing voices and schizophrenic. It's quite amusing yet clever. Caleb came up with that lie. Gina told me he planned to embarrass me by spreading a rumor, creating a Facebook page about me being insane and posting a naked video of me being attacked."

"Wow! Some friends."

"Tell me about it. Just yesterday, he had a friend of mine, Tamara, call me asking for my Facebook password claiming to want to delete my post about the hostage situation since my grandmother's address was in the post."

"Is it possible your friend was being thoughtful?"

"One might think so if they didn't know the history between her and Caleb. She wanted my password to give to him because he planned to post updates as if he were me, posting things to make me seem crazy and schizophrenic. He's done the same thing to his cousin. To this day, he uses her Facebook password to post on her page as if he's her, posting erratic messages that she was raped and taking meds so people will think she's crazy. If anyone is crazy, it's him."

"Wow!"

"Yeah, he's a psychopath. He and my friends were envious of me and intimidated by my success. They hate I moved back here from Philly. My success was a slap in the face for them because it reminded them of where they should be. They said many times I think I'm better than them, but the truth is they feel I am better. I can't help who I am. I worked hard and invested in myself to get where I am. Now they want to take it away."

"Jealously creates hatred and can cause people to become very destructive."

"I see. So anyway, they had a GPS app installed on my phone and tracked me to the Super Food Mart with intent to abduct, kill me and hide my body. It's something they've done before."

"How exactly did you end up here?"

"The Berkley county sheriff suggested I come here for safety since the shelters are not open and secure 24/7. He's the one who told me about this place. I wouldn't have otherwise known."

"The sheriff, huh?"

"Yes"

"I didn't know until after I got here that they installed the app on my phone. I thought they only installed the GPS on my car. So I told the sheriff, I didn't feel comfortable getting back in my vehicle. He told me about the Crisis Center but said they don't normally just bring people here. You have to feel psychotic, not like yourself, or feel like you want to hurt yourself. He basically coached me on what to say to have them transport me here."

After another 30 minutes, the treatment team wanted to order a CAT scan to rule out the possibility of any tumors or disorders, even though they believed the occurrences were real. Documentation of the CAT scan results were needed to support my extended stay in the hospital. I agreed to have it done. Before leaving the meeting room, the doctor said he was going to give me a prescription to take two milligrams of sleeping pills because I had been awake all night. I said OK, but knew I wasn't going to take any of their meds.

I went back to the recliner, worked on a crossword puzzle and rested my eyes. Two and a half hours later, two male attendants arrived with a wheelchair to transport me to radiology for the CAT scan. I didn't know they were coming so soon. I thought it would be at least another day or two. The idea of two strange men transporting me anywhere made me feel uncomfortable.

"Laila, these two gentlemen are here to take you down to X-ray."

"OK, but I would feel much more comfortable with a female attendant. Can you see if a woman is available to take me?"

"A female attendant was requested, but no one was available."

"Oh my goodness. Then can you call security to come and escort us?"

"OK, Laila, if that'll help you feel safe, we'll ask security to come up as well."

A few minutes later, an unarmed security officer came up to accompany us. He looked very young, inexperienced and timid, like he was fresh out of new security officer orientation. He couldn't have weighed more than 150 pounds. His pale face turned red when I told the nurse he wasn't equipped to protect me.

"How is this small, young boy supposed to protect me?"

I wanted the CAT scan rescheduled for a time when a female attendant and female security officer were available. Radiology was booked for the rest of the day, so they wanted this CAT scan done as scheduled. Standing in front of the nurse's station, I negotiated back and forth with the nurse.

"I'm sorry, I really don't feel comfortable going."

"Laila, I promise you, no one is out there waiting for you."

"I know they're still out there waiting to snatch me and whisk me away in their van. They're still parked outside. I really don't feel comfortable. Something doesn't feel right. I'm sorry, I can't go."

"The doctor ordered this CAT scan, and it's really important you go to rule out any tumors or issues."

"Tumors? I don't have a tumor."

"That can only be determined by a CAT scan, which is why you need to go. And we need this documented in your record."

"Hmmm, I'm sorry, I don't feel safe. Look at his face. It's beat red. He's looks nervous, and he's making me feel uncomfortable. I'm not going to risk my life for the pressure of hospital logistics. I'll have to go another time when a female attendant and female security officer are available."

"OK, cancel the appointment," he nurse said. "I apologize for having you guys come up here and wasting your time."

She was visibly frustrated and slammed the door of the nurse's station behind her. I heard the frustration in her voice, but I didn't allow it to make me feel guilty. She was the last person on my mind, and her thoughts of me weren't my worry. My ultimate concern was my safety, and the knot in my stomach commanded me not to go. I refused to ignore my gut. Danger waited to greet me outside the door. They were out there like roaring lions ready to devour me and combat any obstacles that interrupted their plans. Landan had a strong connection to the hospital staff as well as the security team, all of whom had access to my electronic patient records and knew my movements throughout the hospital. Moving around the building would have increased my vulnerability. Rather than walk into a trap, I retreated to the recliner in the hall and stayed right there swaddled in my white hospital blanket.

The doorbell buzzer echoed through the unit once again. There was so much traffic at this spot. People were in and out all day. From the cafeteria workers delivering meals to the unit staff to the cleaning crew and laundry workers, it was a constant flow. Nevertheless, when I heard the buzzer, I darted to the nurse's station to check out the monitor. I recognized the staff member outside the door from the Crisis Center downstairs. She was the person who did my intake. When the aide opened the door for her, two new patients, a male and a female, walked alongside her as she introduced them to the head nurse on duty. After a dry introduction, the new patients were given the procedural handout of slightly used patient scrubs, a patient handbook and a brown paper bag for personal items. They were asked to read the handbook and were escorted to their rooms next door to each other on the other side of the unit.

The staffer sat with them individually and went over the strict rules of the unit, "No cell phones allowed on the floor. We'll need to lock up your jewelry, cash, credit cards, and any other items of value. All your items will be safely stored downstairs with security. You can pick them up when you're discharged. Visiting hours are every day from noon to 2 p.m. and 6-8 p.m. The patient phone is across from the nurse's station on the wall. You are allowed two 30-minute phone calls per day. Meals are served in the dining hall. If you do not complete a menu selection sheet each day, the kitchen will bring you a generic meal for breakfast, lunch, and dinner. There are daily workshops and group therapy sessions that you can attend or you can spend time in the TV room, but all patients must be in their rooms with lights out by 10 p.m. Any questions?"

Her stern voice projected all the way around the corner. To avoid listening to the rest of her painful rules, I reached for the phone next me to call my cousin Stanley. He and I were close in age and grew up together. He was a husky guy with curly black hair and towered me by a foot. During his college years at Florida A&M, he was very athletic and had a promising career with the NFL until he suffered a torn ligament during his senior year. He's not my actual cousin, but we considered each like family since our mothers were so close for over 40 years. His mom was like a dear aunt to me. He was very protective of me; I could always count on him for anything. He knew what I was currently dealing with and knew my friends were after my life insurance policy. He also knew Gina betrayed me with Caleb.

"Hey Stan."

"Hey Laila, how's it going?"

"It's going good. How's it going with you?"

"Pretty good. I was just thinking about you."

"Oh yeah?"

"Yeah, I was. I must tell you I'm really concerned. "

"Concerned? Concerned about what?"

"Well, you know, everything that's going on. You know I believe in you and you know I've got your back. But you have to stay off the phone. You're making all these phone calls."

"Phone calls? What are you talking about?"

"Who've you been calling? You've called the police again."

"What? I haven't called the police since the Crisis Center. I called Mr. Gibson and he called the FBI for me, but I didn't call the police."

"So who else did you call? Who'd you call today?"

"I called a friend of mine. Why?"

"And what did you say to your friend?"

"I told her Caleb, Gina, Tabatha, and Landan conspired to kill me for my life insurance policy. And I asked her if she had a part in it? She said she didn't know what I was talking about and that was it. Oh, yeah, and I told her Brent was in on it too."

"Brent?"

"Yeah. Tabatha said he was still upset about his

windows and have been plotting to retaliate for the last three years."

"Wow. Ain't that a bitch? You know, I heard a while ago that chum wanted to get back at you."

"You did?"

"Yeah. He said something to one of my friends, but this was about two or three years ago so I thought it was over. And there was something he said to Uncle Jimmy before he passed, God bless the dead."

"Are you serious? What did he say?"

"I don't remember his exact words, but basically he wanted to seek revenge."

"Wow, I'm not surprised. He's grimy like that and a snake."

"That no good punk! Don't worry about him, but you've been doing a lot of talking on the phone to people. You have to stay off the phone, Laila. Just stay off the phone."

"Why? What's the problem?"

"You have to be careful who you talk to."

Without him saying specifics, I knew my other girlfriend mentioned my phone call to Tabatha who in turn told Landan. She tells him everything. My frustration grew as Stan became more alarmed with their plot. He sounded jittery, panicky, and out of breath while he made his point clear to stay off the phone. This wasn't the first subliminal message. It was apparent the assailants told him to persuade me to stop talking about the situation to people and to stop calling the police. I'm not easily influenced nor good at following orders. They'd be better off encouraging me to make phone calls to get me to stop. I wasn't going to stop my calls until this was resolved. I learned a long time ago to not negotiate with terrorists, and that's exactly what they were. Terrorists. They terrorized my family, invaded their homes and lives, and threatened them with fear. Unaware of their malicious motives, my family opened the doors of their homes to them because they were friends of mine. Years of trust, friendship and familiarity were the key for entry. Just as with my grandma's house, I detected their voices in the background at Stan's. He had been bullied and threatened. I remained silent because I didn't want him stop giving me the underlying messages, and I needed the assailants to keep feeding him the demands to give me.

code grey

My call to Stan exceeded the allotted time. I usually tried to sneak a few extra minutes if no one was watching, but the nurse's aide came back over for the second time to tell me my time was up. Before Stan hung up, he said how much he loved me and would call me before the phone shut off at 10 p.m. to hear my voice.

"Hear my voice? You sound like it'll be the last time you talk to me."

"No, I didn't say that. I just need to hear your voice tonight before you go to bed Laila."

"Was that another subliminal message?" I asked myself. "Was something going to happen to me where he wouldn't hear my voice tomorrow?"

"OK, Stan, call me before 10."

"OK, love you, Laila."

"Love you too. We'll chat later."

His last comment had me on guard. I thought about it for the rest of the day. I didn't know what to expect, but I was absolutely certain I needed to prepare myself. Before long, the annoying doorbell buzzed again. It sounded like the end of the second quarter of a basketball game. A health aide worker, who was a short but stocky Mexican guy in dark blue hospital scrubs and a leather jacket came in. He wasn't on the clock that shift, so his access card was disabled. He walked around the corner to the nurse's station, chatted for less than a minute to the nurse, and grabbed a clipboard with the list of patients. He flipped through the pages on the clipboard, hung it back up, and marched down the hall. Halfway down the hall, he stopped to read the list of the day's events on the bulletin board, then continued to parade down the hall around the back side of the unit back near me. While he walked toward the door, he stopped and stared directly in my eyes, and firmly nodded his head to assert he knew who I was.

I wasn't sure what to make of his gesture, but it was intimidating. I walked to the nurse's aide and asked a few questions about him. She told me he worked for the hospital a long time and occasionally covered this floor. Something about him and his march around the unit didn't seem right.

"Why did he give me the head nod like that?" I wondered. He was on the floor no more than five minutes, wasn't working that night but had obviously come for a purpose. I needed to jot this down with my other notes. I was keeping a daily log of almost everything that occurred during my stay. I darted to my room to grab my blue folder from the middle drawer. I had so much on my mind, and I surely didn't want to forget him or his unusual behavior. I knew it would eventually mean something and later come in handy.

After journaling about him, I went into the dining hall with the other residents to eat lunch. This was the first time I had eaten since I'd been in the hospital. I didn't want to enjoy the pleasures of food while my family was held against their will and possibly starving. I sat at the table with a guy and an older woman with silver hair who often loudly erupted singing Christmas and spiritual medleys. She had a high-pitched screeching, off-key voice and adlibbed most of the words. The guy at the table tried his hardest to keep from laughing. Her singing was annoying, but we endured it because of her old age.

The doorbell buzzed again. By the time I ran from the dining hall to the nurse's station to check the monitor, the visitor had already been let in by the nurse.

"Hi, I'm here as a volunteer for the AA meeting."

"Oh, OK. What time does the meeting start?"

"Three o'clock"

"OK, come on in. The meeting is held in the corner conference room. Down the hall, take a right, and it's the first room on your right."

"OK, thanks."

"Wait, he's not a volunteer!" I shouted to the nurse. He doesn't even have a visitor or volunteer badge. Where's his badge?"

"Laila, please go sit down. He is a volunteer. I've seen him here before with the coordinator who leads the AA group. They're here every week and the coordinator is on his way."

"Yeah, I'm sure they are here every week but not him. I read in the hospital handbook all volunteers have to check in at the front desk and get a volunteer badge. He doesn't have a badge."

"I left my badge at home," he told the nurse.

"It's OK. The group leader hasn't arrived yet but will be here shortly."

"It's not OK. He's lying. Don't believe him. He's not supposed to be here."

"Laila, please sit down."

"No, I'm not going to sit down because you're allowing him to violate the hospital policy. He's an intruder."

The nurse ushered me back to the dining room, but I snuck out as soon as she turned the corner. The volunteer was a tall, thin man, wore a fitted black skullcap and black pea coat, and he hadn't shaved in days. He carried a recyclable mesh Walmart bag with the straps wrapped tightly around his wrist. The bulky item inside seemed to weigh down the bag.

Strolling a few feet behind the supposed volunteer, I asked, "What's in the bag?"

"The good stuff," he said bluntly as he walked into the corner meeting room and shut the door behind him.

"Yeah, I bet it is."

I peeped through the door's corner glass to see what he was going to do with the bag. After taking his coat off, he placed the bag on the floor near the trash can along the back wall. He walked toward the door, so I darted around the corner to pretend I was coming out of the hall bathroom near the entrance. I walked to the dining area, and he came in a few steps after me looking for a stack of coffee cups. He was pretending to set up the room for the facilitator but he wasn't fooling me. Once the group leader arrived, he announced the AA meeting was ready to get underway and anyone who was interested could attend. Three patients joined the meeting including the new guy who had been admitted less than an hour before. His leg cast forced him to walk with a limp. He wore a religious cap, sported a goatee and had a noticeable breathing disorder. He walked into the meeting room and sat next to the volunteer. There were only five people seated at a table for 10.

"Why would he sit directly next to the mysterious guy?" I asked myself. The volunteer noticed me watching him and seemed to be a bit nervous. He quickly glanced away as soon we made eye contact and pretended to tune in to the discussion. I continued to stare at him through the glass to see if it would get a rise out of him. He became fidgety and so uncomfortable that he jumped out his seat. I also jumped because I thought he was coming toward me at the door but he moved to the opposite side of the man he was sitting next to. I waited a few minutes longer by the door and shortly strolled down the hall to the TV room to watch the Wheel of Fortune. But I couldn't focus on the show while so much ran through my mind. The running washing machine in the laundry room next door created more of a distraction.

The TV room had plush old-fashioned wooden chairs arranged theater-style facing the outdated television. Worn-down novels and boxes of jigsaw puzzles with missing pieces surrounded the TV on the built-in book shelf. The large window in back of us added a shivering chill to the room. After 40 minutes, the man with the goatee walked in and sat a few seats from me on the opposite side of the room.

"The meeting is over already?" I asked.

"No, it's still going on. They're getting ready to wrap up. They only have a few minutes left."

"Oh, OK, why'd you come out?"

"I was getting tired of listening to it, and I only sat in there to kill some time. Nothing else to do here."

"Yeah, I hear ya. That tall white guy sitting near the group leader, was he a volunteer?"

"The one that had the black hat on?"

"Yeah"

"That's Jack."

"You know him?"

"Yeah, I know him from the old neighborhood from back in the day. He used to live in my building."

"Really?"

"Was he a volunteer?"

"Uh, is that what he said?"

"That's what he told the nurse."

"I don't know. I guess so if that's what he said."

"Something didn't seem right about that man."

"Why you say that?"

"First of all, he came on the floor without a badge. All volunteers wear badges. He was acting weird, like he was nervous about something. He just seemed like a fish out of water. He was carrying a large bulky item in his bag. Looked like it could have been a gun."

"A gun? Why you think that?"

"Something in my spirit tells me. He was completely out of place here, like he doesn't belong as part of that group."

"Why you so nervous about him? What's going on? You think someone is after you?"

"I know it."

"Is that why you're here?"

"Yep"

"Because you think someone is after you?"

"Yep, sure do."

"But why you think that?"

"Because my friends — well, former friends — are trying to kill me."

"Kill you? For what? Do you have some information on them?"

"No! For my life insurance policy."

"Your life insurance policy?"

"The guy I was dating found out my best friend was the executor and trustee of my Will and forged a relationship with her to manipulate her for my policy."

"Wow, how much is it worth?"

"A half million dollars plus assets and real estate."

"Damn, you're worth more to them dead than alive, huh?"

"I guess so."

"What are your friends' names?"

"You don't know them."

"You don't know who I know."

"I'm not telling you."

"Did you tell the staff here that someone is trying to kill you?"

"Yes."

"And what happened, they didn't believe you?"

"No"

"They think you're crazy, huh?"

"Yeah. They believed me at first, but now they say it's a delusion."

"You ain't crazy. That shit is real."

The nurse interrupted our conversation, "Laila, if it makes you feel better, the group meeting is over and everyone from the outside has left."

"Well, it's about time."

Eager to end my conversation with the man with the goatee, I got up and walked down the hall to the meeting room. I wanted to see if that mesh bag was still by the trash can where the guy placed it. When I got to the room, the door was locked and the lights were off. Through the glass in the door, I saw the bag was gone, but something made me think its contents were still in the room. He could have passed whatever was in that bag underneath the table to his childhood buddy. Interesting that they knew each other from middle school and the same neighborhood. This put me more on edge. How did he know the staff didn't believe me? I wondered.

"How did he know anything about me?" I wondered. Why would he say, "This is real" and that I'm "Worth more to them dead than I am alive?" For someone to just arrive and never have met me, he knew an awful lot. He seemed to know people were after me and trying to kill me. His questions weren't typical. They weren't random. He definitely knew something. However, I couldn't prove it. But I was sure that moving forward I couldn't trust him and needed to keep an eye on him at all times.

I stayed near the meeting room leaning against the wall thinking until the kitchen staff came in the unit.

They wheeled in a large heated dining cart stacked with our dinner trays. Each person chose two entrees, two sides, dessert, and a drink. I hadn't eaten in several days and decided I'd better get some real food into my system. I ordered a cheeseburger, French fries, broccoli, hot tea and lemon meringue pie. Walking behind the cart, I grabbed my tray and sat next the old lady.

"Laila, you're so beautiful honey."

"Thank you, ma'am."

"God loves you."

"God loves you too."

I tried to keep my head down and avoid eye contact because she wouldn't stop talking once she started and then she'd break into a song. I heard enough of her singing to last a lifetime and didn't want to give her the impression that I wanted to hear her talking, let alone singing. Avoiding eye contact didn't help. I pretended to pay attention and seem interested in what she was saying. I was interested, however, to know why she thought her son was Satan and referred to him as Lucifer when they spoke on the phone. During one of their calls, she nearly performed an exorcism on him.

"Lucifer, you get the fuck outta there. Get the fuck outta my son's body, you fucking devil. Satan, get the fuck out of my house. In the precious name of Jesus, I rebuke you, Satan. Get out, get out." She shouted at the top of her lungs before the nursing staff came to calm her down. Her using cuss words in the same sentence with Jesus was a bit unorthodox. We knew not to say anything to her about it because she nearly cursed out the last person who did. It was hard to imagine this 70-year-old woman speaking the way she did, especially after singing spiritual songs all day.

I just sat there at the table while she talked, and talked. The guy with the goatee looked up at me from across the room and asked me to come to his table for a second. I was reluctant to do so because I didn't trust him. After pointing to myself, in a "who me?" kind of way to make sure it was me he was gesturing, I slowly walked over.

"Yeah, what's up?"

"I meant to tell you, I like your hoodie. Can I touch it? What is this, Velcro?"

"Velcro? Don't you mean velvet like the line in 'Coming to America'?"

"Yeah, that's what I meant. My bad."

"No, it's fleece."

"Oh, OK, I got one just like it."

"Oh, yeah."

"Let me feel it."

"This guy can't seriously be interested in feeling my fleece hoodie. What is wrong with him?" I asked myself.

"I like this. This feels nice."

He started digging down his cast to scratch his leg. For the second time, he wanted to smoke and needed a lighter. He said he had one in his cast and started to dig for it. "Why would he need a lighter in this non-smoking building?" It's not like he can voluntarily walk off the unit or even open the secure metal door.

"You still think somebody is trying to kill you?"

"Yeah, I do."

"Do you really think that guy had a gun?"

"Yep, I really do."

"Do you think I have a gun?"

"What?"

He asked me this at the same time as digging further down his cast.

"Oh, my God, he has a gun! He has a gun!"

Everyone in the room went into a panic. Those seated nearby slid their chairs back away from the table; others ran out to the hall. The nursing staff heard the panic and dashed into the dining hall.

"What's wrong? What's going on in here?"

"He has a gun."

"What?"

"He has a gun in his cast."

"I don't have a gun."

"Yes he does, check his cast. Check him."

"Laila, calm down. He doesn't have a gun."

"Yes, he does. Then check him, if you think he doesn't have a gun."

"No one can get a gun on the floor past security."

"Check him."

"Laila, why don't you take a moment in your room? You're not thinking clearly right now and your outbursts are disrupting the other patients."

"I'm not going anywhere."

The nurse tried to calm me down. Everyone was so focused on me that they missed him put something in the bottom cabinet under the sink before he walked back to the table.

"He just put something under the sink. You need to check it out."

"Laila, I'm warning you."

"Call security if you're not going to check it out yourself."

The nurse walked into the nurse's station while the other staff members stayed in the dining hall to calm the others down.

"So you're not going to call security or address the concern."

"Laila, please calm down."

"Fine, I'll call myself."

I picked up the patient phone on the wall.

"Hello, Security, how may I help you?"

"We need security on M5."

"Is this a Code Grey?"

"Hmmm, it can be?"

"Wait, what? Are you a patient or a nurse?

"I'm a patient, and we need security. There's a patient up here with a gun."

"I'm going to hang up and call the nurse's desk."

I saw the nurse reach to answer the phone when it rang in her area. I didn't hear what she said to the caller, but within seconds a woman's voice abruptly announced an urgent code over the hospital's intercom.

"Code Grey, female, M5. I repeat, Code Grey, female, M5."

Available staff from every floor rushed to the unit. Literally, within less than two minutes, 15 staffers — security personnel, nurses and health aides — responded to the hospital security code. The head nurse briefed them on what happened. I tried to listen, but I couldn't hear their whisper.

"Listen, I called you guys because the man in there with the goatee had a gun in his cast."

"He does not have a gun."

"She didn't even search him."

"Laila, I need you to go to your room now. Please go to your room."

"Not until you search him."

"Laila, if you don't go into your room, we're going to have to give you medication intravenously, two injections in each arm."

"Are you kidding me?"

"No, I'm not."

"But you didn't even check him?"

"OK, Laila that's it."

The nurse had two security officers usher me to my room and onto on my bed while a sea of hospital staffers surrounded my room. One of the aides sat on the bed next to me while the nurse stood over me with two hypodermic needles.

"I can't believe this is happening."

"This is going to help you relax. It will put you to sleep within 45 minutes."

"What? I don't want to go to sleep? I need to stay up to watch what's going on around me."

"You'll be fine."

"I don't want to go to sleep, and I don't want to sleep in this room by myself."

"You're not going to be alone. For the first 45 minutes, the aide will sit in the chair by the door. You're going to be fine. Just be still because this one is going to sting a little. It'll be a little sore tomorrow, but you'll be OK."

Right after that needle, she gave me another needle in the other arm. It seemed like something I'd seen in a movie. So many things happened since I been in the hospital were like they'd been written in a film script. I tried to stay alert to avoid falling asleep. It was getting late and I didn't want to be in this room alone, certainly not for the entire night. I have no idea when I fell asleep but the medication must have had an immediate affect. All I remember is asking the aide her name, how long she been there and if she could stay longer than 45 minutes. She assured me she'd stay beyond 45 minutes as long as she could.

By the time I realized I'd been sleeping, three hours had passed. I jumped out of bed, snatched my blanket and rushed around the corner to get to the hallway recliner. Normally, I'd push back in the chair to lie back with my feet propped but this time I wanted to sit straight up with my feet on the floor to stay awake throughout the night to watch out for the man with the goatee. He and a woman checked themselves in. So much had happened on the unit. I needed to keep a watchful eye on the two posing as patients, who were in fact hired to kill me in the hospital. Those two were clearly in cahoots with the man pretending to be the AA volunteer.

another failed attempt

Mornings in the hospital were routine and dull. The lack of color and character from the walls added to the monotony. Nothing seemed to brighten or enliven the place. The deep undertone of stress, anguish, and anxiety on the unit absorbed pleasant thoughts. Many times it absorbed all thoughts to where you didn't have a thought at all — just a paralyzing empty calmness — while you tried to conjure up a thought. Since each day was routine with nothing to look forward to, anticipation of the drawn-out hours evaporated in the air of boredom.

The morning light filtered through the cloudy grey sky as the patients were awakened by the 6:45 a.m. shift change. In the nurse's common area down the hall, the staff debriefed each other before scattering to the patient rooms with portable blood pressure stands in tow. The squeaking and rolling of the five-wheeled apparatus meant she was near. Whether you were asleep or otherwise, she'd abruptly interrupt. I was lying back in the hall recliner when the nurse walked up to me.

"Good morning, Laila."

"Good morning."

"How are you this morning?"

"Tired."

"Well, I just need to check your vitals. Then you can continue to rest."

"All right."

"I just need your right arm, sweetie."

She wrapped the blood pressure cuff around my upper arm and securely tightened the Velcro. As she rapidly squeezed the bulb from the 8-inch coiled tubing, the cuff tightened on my arm with intensity. It was so tight that I thought my arm was going to explode.

"Ouch, that's really tight."

"Oh wow, I'm sorry, Laila. It looks like someone changed the gauge on the pressure to read a larger arm. I'll change it. I'll need to start over."

"Just great."

"Almost finished."

With the one twist of the valve the air rapidly released, sounding similar to helium releasing from a filled balloon. For a moment, I almost forgot where I was since it sounded so much like a carnival's balloon station.

"Ok, Laila, just need to take your pulse and temperature, and then we're all set."

"OK."

"All right, everything looks good," she said as she snatched the cuff from the Velcro to remove it from my arm. "Your pressure's 118 over 78, and your pulse is 62. Both are very good. You're all set, so you can go back to sleep now if you want."

"I wish I could. I'm wide awake now."

Just about everyone on the floor was awake. I'm not sure how anyone could go back to sleep after the torture of the blood pressure cuff around their arm. Plus, the clatter and chatter of the nurses moving about on the floor with those squeaky wheels while talking to the patients was enough to keep anyone up.

Vitals, 8 a.m. breakfast and a hot shower were the normal routine. After that, patients received a number to indicate their turn in line for the motion censored shower. They grabbed their change of clothes and pink basins filled with soap, shampoo, and deodorant, and stood in line outside the hall shower. I usually tried to be one of the first in line since I hated waiting around.

This time, I was fourth. There were two private showers next door to each other.

The doors locked from the outside and could only be opened by hospital staff. In the hall were metal carts stacked with brittle towels and washcloths that were harsh against your skin. Other toiletries were also in the cart placed outside the doors. Two aides, male and female, sat in a chair outside the door to hand out towels, washcloths, and soap. If you wanted to shave while in the shower, they provided a generic razor and waited outside the shower curtain until you handed the razor back to them. Diligently they'd inspect the razor to make sure the blade and clear cap were still attached. Likewise, they monitored the 15-minute shower time. "Five more minutes," they'd shout before turning the shower off themselves outside the door.

Even though I was fourth in line, I was still paranoid and cautious of the two suspicious-looking patients who checked themselves in. They were two positions behind me. I was apprehensive about getting in the shower and felt I'd be safer taking a sponge bath. The male aide outside the shower was the same off-duty Mexican guy who walked by me the other day, stared directly in my eyes and firmly nodded. I didn't feel comfortable with him and the two culprits outside the door. With the three of them together there, I was not going to turn my back and stand vulnerable in the shower while the Mexican guy had the key.

"All right, Laila, your turn," the female aide said.

"My turn? I'm not sure I want to go in right now. I don't feel comfortable."

"What's the problem now, Laila?"

"He makes me feel uncomfortable" I said as I pointed to the male aide.

"Humberto?"

"Yes."

"Laila, he's working. He's been here a long time and is very good with the patients."

"I'm not getting in right now. Can you call another female aide to sit in his place while I shower?"

"Here we go again. It's just him and me working this morning."

"Well, it's my patient right to request someone else, and you cannot deny me of my rights. Please call the nurse manager to get someone else, and let me know when they're here. I'll be in dining hall."

"I'll call someone, but I need to stay here until everyone has showered. I'll call then, and I cannot guarantee it will be this morning that someone will be able to relieve him. It may be this afternoon before lunch", she said while shaking her head.

"That's fine with me. I can wait."

"OK, Laila."

She rolled her eyes and shook her head before pointing to the next person in line to move toward the shower. Humberto had a surprised yet disgusted look on his face. He seemed upset that their rehearsed plan was interrupted. He wasn't aware that I was on to him although my outburst and suspicion of him were obvious. He was very mysterious and I was certain he had a part in the conspiracy. I had my eye on him ever since I noticed him on the unit the day before. His purpose was twofold. One, to confirm I was still there, and two, to advise the AA volunteer imposter of the listed activities to help set the stage to perform their scripted murderous act.

Like Humberto, the phony male and female patients too looked disappointed while they stood in line with their basins watching me walk away. The plan was to bombard the bathroom and attack me in the shower. They would wait three minutes after I went into the shower allowing time for me to get undressed. The woman was to distract the female aide by initiating a disturbance with another patient down the hall, knowing the aide would rush to control the situation. While the other patients stayed in line and staff members attended to the disturbance more than 200 feet away, the male conspirator would slip into the shower room. Humberto was then to immediately lock the door to prevent me from escaping.

Wrapped in his bundled clothes, the fake patient had a pair of latex gloves and a sharp makeshift knife. He stayed up through the night mastering this craft and refining a long-handled toothbrush into a weapon.

Since the toothbrush had a thick rubber grip, he removed the bristles from the narrower end which he scraped and chiseled against the bathroom's concrete wall. To mute the scraping sound, he placed two rolled towels across the bottom of the hollow bathroom door. In between chiseling, he repeatedly applied heat from the radiator to shape its point before it cooled and then filed some more.

Filing the handle to a sharp spear point without causing it to break was a tedious and meticulous task. He also had to be careful to not get caught. Every 15 minutes he dashed to his bed just before the nurse made her rounds. After she peeked in the room and noticed him asleep, he darted back to the bathroom and continued scraping. A few times, he was so immersed in making the shank that he lost track of time, leaving him to fool the nurse that he was in the bathroom with an upset stomach.

"You OK in there?"

"Hmmmm, no, my stomach is sick. I ate something my stomach doesn't agree with."

"Oh wow. Would you like me to get you anything?"

"No thank you, I'll be OK. It's been going on all night, but I'll be fine."

"OK, I'll check on you during my next round," she softly said as she cracked the door.

"OK, thank you."

He was just as good at fooling the nurse as he was in making the make-shift knife. He played the sick role like an award-winning actor, moaning and groaning, and clenching his stomach while sitting on the toilet seat. As soon as she walked away, he'd let go of his stomach and resume chiseling until the toothbrush had a piercing sharp edge. He was relentless about getting this done to perfection. When he was finished he had created a deadly weapon in one the city's reputedly securest hospitals without detection.

As he stood in line, the makeshift knife was secured in his bundled clothes, wrapped in the leg of his pant scrubs. He held the clothes tight against his chest to ensure the weapon didn't drop out. Just before Humberto was to unlock the door to let him slip out the shower room, he was to stab me in the chest, clean the handle and carefully place the knife in my right hand to give the impression of a suicide. In his bundled clothes, he also carried an old T-shirt to clean up the splattered blood in effort to sidetrack the crime-scene investigators from detecting foul play. He knew evidence of blood splatter could be inconsistent with self-inflicted wounds since they generally don't leave the same gruesome trail of blood splatter as a cold-blooded attack. As knowledgeable, prepared and criminal-minded as they were, their suspicious behavior foiled their own elaborate and devious scheme.

They felt defeated and humiliated, and were embarrassed to tell their pseudo urban guerilla LJ I escaped the snared trap once again. Dare they explain how I disarmed and disabled them a second time without physically stripping them of their armor? I did, however, strip them of their macho, dignity and pride. Shaking them and walking away without a scratch was like a brilliant move in the NBA. They had the ball in their court with me on defense. I faked a move to the right prompting them to go left as I intended, giving me the opportunity to snatch the dribbled ball and land a glorious three-point shot in their face. With my hands still extended in the air from the shot, "swish" was the sound I made while silence swept the crowd — just as when I walked away from the shower leaving the fake patients in the line trying to figure out what just happened. The look on their faces was priceless. They were in awe and disbelief.

The embarrassment and expected ridicule was at an all-time high, and their anger kept growing. They were not going to let me keep getting away. Besides, the stakes for my life increased with the little time left on the expiring policy. Only three days remained. For this reason, they were determined to prove themselves as aggressive enforcers and take the upper hand. Cashing in on the lucrative deal was a powerful driving force. To accomplish this, they concocted and rehearsed yet another scheme. The blueprint, exact timeline and participants were all defined. In their eyes, this was the be-all and end-all of master plans. They came up with a completely different strategy for an attack. They ditched the makeshift knife and swore this would be my last night alive.

their clever plan

Seth and Caleb were military buddies, having spent 15 years together during their overseas deployment in Germany, Afghanistan, and Iraq as well as stateside at Fort Benning, Georgia. Caleb had manipulated his way to the Special Force Operations unit by sleeping with one of the high-ranking blondes. In Special Ops, he executed raids, deactivated land mines, descended from helicopters into hostile territories and gathered foreign intelligence. He acquired high-level tactics in counter-terrorism, psychological operations, manhunts, and unorthodox warfare, skills he transferred to his combative civilian life after the army. He knew all the ins and outs, and he was a master at starting, finishing, and escaping trouble.

Seth's role was a dangerous one as well. He was part of an infantry unit on the front line, fighting face-to-face with the enemy. He received special training in espionage and counterintelligence. Like Caleb, he manipulated these military skills into his malicious civilian life. Both men received a dishonorable discharge for murdering an unarmed fellow soldier. They claimed the incident was the result of friendly fire while ambushing the enemy, but that was nothing more than a cover-up. They knew the military would have a difficult time proving otherwise. A week before the killing, Caleb had a physical altercation with the soldier, and their other fellow soldiers who witnessed it were afraid to blow the whistle. They knew Caleb, a well-trained boxer, was ruthless and would spare them no mercy if any one of them opened their mouth.

Caleb became infuriated when the small-framed soldier slapped him across the face. His first instinct was to punch the guy, drop him to the ground and stomp on his chest. It was no secret Caleb had a violent temper and destructive hands. He swung so fast you could barely see his fists coming. The smallest issue would anger him, but this time he decided to retreat to his barracks and devise a demonic game plan. He pretended to let it go, swallow his pride, and keep calm while he formulated a strategy for revenge. He wanted the soldier dead and knew Seth was just the person to enlist as his accomplice to go to war against the object of his rage.

After serving on the catastrophic battlefields of Afghanistan and Iraq, Seth suffered post-traumatic stress disorder. To compound his misery, shortly after coming home from Afghanistan, he tragically lost his wife in a fatal car crash, and he hadn't been the same since. His return was the start of many postwar battles.

He had sporadic violent episodes which were managed, though only barely, by daily medication. He felt he had no reason to live, no one to live for, and he simply wanted out. Coupled with bipolar disorder and daily drinking binges, Seth was a walking time bomb. His life spiraled out of control. Caleb knew Seth had an explosive temper, was easily angered, and walked around with an I-don't-give-a-fuck attitude.

So he hired Seth as the hit man, which allowed him to keep his hands clean. That was one of his life mottos. With myriad other undeniable mental health issues on top of PTSD and being bipolar, Seth could easily get himself admitted to the hospital's psychiatric ward. His girlfriend had her own mental illnesses, so to join him for the ride she checked herself in too. They anticipated getting the job done in two days and checking themselves out in record time before anyone caught on to their conspiracy. Their plan of staying in the hospital for only two nights failed but they were forced to stay a little longer to finish the assignment. If they failed to do so, they would have to return the up-front money Caleb advanced them. Since neither Seth nor his girlfriend had a job and Seth was disqualified by the Veterans Administration for benefits, they were broke, desperate for money and determined to do whatever it took to close the murderous deal.

Southern Coastal Hospital, particularly its M5 unit, was supposed to be one of the most secure hospitals in the South. The top administrators and other hospital personnel had no idea such corruption was unfolding right under their noses.

To the mentally unstable couple, it was business as usual. Unbelievable. Then again, I could believe it. Gina's seven-month fling with Caleb reminded me anything's possible and anything could unfold under your nose without having the slightest clue. Some people can be very sneaky and go to great lengths to avoid getting caught, even if it means doing something dastardly right in your face and compromising their integrity, values, and liberty.

I was, however, surprised Seth and his girlfriend would go to the extent of checking themselves into a psych ward to engage in a deadly plot against a stranger. Money will make some people do the darndest things. There was a big bounty on my proverbial head, and the premium doubled as the insurance policy's expiration date approached. It was three days away. My would-be assailants were anxious to bring this to an end to get the balance of their payout, and head home for their neighbor's New Year's Eve party.

Still leaning along the wall across from the shower room, they watched me in disgust as I strolled down the hallway. The mortified look on their faces spoke volumes. They were angry that I had been able to get away, yet again. If looks could kill, they could have collected the bounty right then and there.

When I turned the corner, the breakfast trays were on the kitchen counter. I grabbed mine. It was still a little warm. I figured I'd go to the dining hall to eat. I had time to kill, so to speak. I wasn't comfortable showering with Humberto on duty, and it would be a couple of hours until a different aide came on the floor to replace him.

The elderly woman was sitting at the table with an art therapist. As part of the therapy, the counselor gave everyone a sheet from a preschooler's coloring book to create a masterpiece of Little Miss Muffet.

"Hi, beautiful, why don't you sit down and join me?" the still-talkative elderly lady asked.

"I sure will, as soon as I finish making my phone call."

I had no intentions on sitting with her again. She was very sweet but also very annoying. The last time I was with her, she sang at the top of her lungs, performed an exorcism on her son, and talked my ears off. She was an attention whore. I had too much on my mind to deal with her nonsense. So to avoid her, I picked up the phone to call Stan.

"Hello."

"Hey, Stan, how are you?"

"Hey, Laila, what's going on?"

"What isn't going on?"

"What do you mean?"

"Well for starters, two patients checked themselves into the hospital posing as patients when in fact they were hired to carry out the hit on me."

"What the ...?!"

"Yes. I came here to feel safe, and now I have no peace. I have to freakin' watch my back because they're always planning something."

"Are you sure that pair is there for you?"

"Yes, it's a man and a woman. They came in together, and nothing is wrong with them. The guy is actually a former military buddy of Caleb's, and he's just as crazy and violent as Caleb. Another of their accomplices had a gun in here yesterday."

"What?"

"Yeah. Caleb's buddy got it from this man posing as an AA meeting volunteer here on the unit. He fabricated a great story, pretended they were middle-school friends, and orchestrated a plan to kill me right here in the hospital."

"Where are you now in the hospital?"

"I'm on the unit, using the patient phone?"

"And where are they?"

"They were both back in line to get in the shower. They were behind me, waiting for me to get in the shower so they could carry out their plan."

"What?"

"Yes, it's crazy. I'm came here to feel safe, to have peace, and to think my situation through. But I can barely sleep. I've been in constant paranoia since I've been here."

"So what are you going to do, Laila?"

"I have no idea. I'm going to have to get out of here somehow."

"What do you mean?"

"I mean break out of here, freakin' escape. I have no choice."

"No, you can't do that."

"Why not?"

"Where would you go? It's freezing outside."

"I have no idea, but I have to get out of here."

"Laila, just cancel your life insurance policy since that's what they're after."

"I didn't even think of that. I've been so busy trying to counter their attacks and plan ahead. I'm about to call my job now to speak to HR."

"OK, call me back when you're done."

"OK, thanks, Stan. Love you."

"Love you too, Lay."

With just three days left on the policy, I never even thought to cancel it. I couldn't believe this was something I had to go through, nor that I had to call my job to cancel my policy. After hanging up with Stan, I made several attempts to reach our corporation's HR department. Several people in the office were on vacation so it was difficult to reach a live person. After several attempts, I called my local office to speak to the assistant. He and I were good friends, and I was comfortable telling him the truth along with the urgency to terminate the policy.

"Good morning, Coastal Pharmaceutical Laboratories, how can I direct your call?"

"Can I speak to Human Resources please?"

"Sure, can I tell them who is calling?"

"Laila Roberts."

"One moment please."

"Hi, Laila, how are you?"

"Hey, Connor, how are you?"

"I'm good, happy holidays."

"Thanks. Happy holidays to you as well. Connor, I wanted to find out a few things regarding my life insurance policy."

"OK, let me pull up your employee profile in our database. What information do you need?"

"How much is my policy?"

"Give me one second while my system loads?"

"OK."

"My system's has been running slow all morning."

"Well, I know how that can be. That's happened to me many times."

"OK, my system pulled up. What information do you need?"

"First, I would like to know the amount of my life insurance policy."

"It looks that you've taken advantage of Part A and Option B. With the two combined, your total policy is $500,000."

"That's what I thought. What do I have to do to cancel it?"

"It's interesting you called inquiring about your policy because one of your family members called today as well asking questions about your policy. I hope you don't plan to use this anytime soon?"

"One of my family members called asking my life insurance?"

"Yes"

"Who?"

"I'm not exactly sure. It was a gentleman. Because he's not listed on the policy, we couldn't release any information to him."

"Wow! That's bizarre. Well, I need to cancel my policy right away."

"Again, does this have anything to the call I received regarding your policy?"

"I'm not sure, I just know I need to cancel my policy."

"I'll contact the policy administrator but I don't believe it's that simple because it's not open enrollment period. It's also going to be hard to reach someone since many people are on holiday vacations. I'll give you a call back this afternoon."

"Great, let me give you a different number to reach me on."

As he researched the information on canceling the policy, I paced back and forth along the hallway to think this through. I was blinded by fake smiles, fake hugs, and fake friends — plus now possibly even my family based on the mysterious call the HR director received from a relative of mine. There's no reason anyone in my family should contact my employer about my policy, unless they needed to call to submit a death claim. Even so, in the event something untoward did happen to me, a male family member was never appointed, authorized nor assigned that role. I purchased the policy as security for my family; ironically, it's being twisted into the very thing that could cost me my life.

As the evening progressed, I sat on the edge of my bed pondering the possible outcomes. The few things Seth said to me made it seem like this could have been my last day. I thought about an escape through the side back door that led to a stairway. I had no idea where it wound up, but I considered just busting the door open, running down to the lower level and out to the door to the snowy street in my yellow patient socks. At least I had my fleece hooded jacket on and figured I'd be warm enough until I found a shelter. Several staff members were in the dining hall, so I crept down the hallway hoping no one would hear or see me. I pushed the stainless steel emergency handle, and an alarm went off. What's more, the door was still locked, and I remained on the floor. I quickly walked away as the staff raced to disable the sounding alarm.

After several hours, a female aide finally came to chaperone me as I got into the shower. It was a nice break in the evening and a great way to rest my mind. The hot water was both soothing and exhilarating. I stood directly under the nozzle as the water cascaded from the top of my head, over my face, and down my legs. It felt like a tropical outdoor shower in Maui. Even though no one waited to shower after me, the aide still restricted me to the 15-minute limit. I begged her for five additional minutes in the shower since I wasn't ready to escape the flow of my imagined exotic island shower. But she refused to oblige and instead issued a harsh warning before abruptly shutting the shower off.

after midnight

Sleeping in the recliner became increasingly uncomfortable but I endured the hardship because I refused to doze off in my room. Several times I asked for a roommate, but the nurse felt my antics on safety would cause disruption. So I settled for sleeping in the hallway chair. The day had been tiring, long and grueling. I had so much on my mind and didn't get my usual catnaps, which made me extremely exhausted. My eyes were weary, and I felt myself drifting off. As tired as I was, I was determined to stay awake through the night. I was my own watch commander and had to remain on duty. As the night progressed, I let down my guard. The evening shower and silence on the floor had tranquilized me. Before I knew it I was fast asleep.

Several nights passed, and since nothing had physically happened to me, I came to trust the nurses' encouragement to get some rest. I was reluctant but knew my body needed it. I woke up once or twice. Each time I poked my head around to glimpse the nurses working in their station. Reassured of their presence, I decided it was time to finally sleep until morning. Just as I was comfortably resting, I sensed the presence of someone approaching me and felt the vibration of someone tiptoeing a few feet away. I slowly opened my eyes. Seth's girlfriend, Anita, was standing over me with a hypodermic needle in her hand. It was aimed directly at me. Immediately I sat up and stared at her as if to say, "What the hell are you doing?" My silent demand worked. She quickly pivoted toward the chair next to me and sat there as if that were her initial plan.

I realized this woman had to be out of her mind. She tried to make small talk as if I didn't just see what she had in her hand, and what she would have done if I hadn't awoken. But she wasn't sure if I saw the needle and thought sparking a conversation would be a great way to read me, so I played along. She was cunning but fake. Her shadiness reminded me of Gina, who was even more trifling then her. They both were a mirror of the injured snake in the story with the Good Samaritan who gained the trust of the innocent through deception, and pulled them in close enough to bite 'em. Neither women could be trusted. There are two ways to deal with a snake: Avoid it or kill it, and I was going to avoid Anita while keeping a watchful eye on her sneaky ways.

Anita scored at deception. During the Code Grey fiasco when Seth had the gun, she gained access to the nurse's locked medicine cabinet and stole two vials of Propofol, a potent drug used for surgical anesthesia. A few hours prior to sneaking up on me, she filled the syringe with the two vials to inject me as I slept in the chair in the middle of the night. Anita knew doubling the dosage would be lethal especially with my egg allergy. Somehow she reviewed my file and discovered I was allergic to eggs. Propofol contained 1.2 percent purified egg phospholipid as an emulsifier, and this active agent along with the high dosage would cause cardiac arrest and ultimately death. She planned to slip back into her room undetected, leaving the needle in my hand to create the appearance of a self-injected overdose. By the time the toxicology report would have been released, both of my assailants would have been discharged and home celebrating the New Year. My death would have been ruled a suicide. It was a clever plan, which they probably would have gotten away with it, but once again their demonic scheme was interrupted.

I'd played it cool with her and her manic boyfriend, Seth, long enough. Enough was enough, and I needed to say something, so I turned to her and asked, "Were you just about to inject me with that needle?"

"Pardon me? What needle?"

"Listen, lady, please don't play games. I saw the needle in your hand."

"I didn't have a needle in my handle. Perhaps you're seeing things? I heard you were hearing voices. Maybe you're also seeing things."

"Really, lady? Please don't challenge my intelligence."

She was pissing me off, but I remained calm and kept a low tone because I didn't want to cause a scene or alert the nursing staff. I had to be careful because I didn't want them to call another Code Grey, and forcibly inject and sedate me again. But I was determined to get to the bottom of this once and for all.

"Are you here as part of the plot to kill me?"

"No, baby, I'm not."

Just like Gina she lied with a straight face. She had a quirky smirk that told it all. I didn't press the issue. It's pointless to debate with liars. It's best to let them believe they have the upper hand and then slowly strip them of their power. Yet I also wanted her to know I was on to the both of them and planned to watch them for the rest of their stay.

She was unmoved by my suspicion and stayed in the chair a few minutes longer before reaching for the phone. Even though it was after the 10 p.m. cutoff for calls, she was able to sneak one in. I wasn't sure who she was talking to but she clearly spoke about me in killer code language.

"Hey, it's me," she whispered. "I wasn't able to get the food in the microwave, but I'll finish before daybreak. Yeah, once it goes in it will be done in 30-60 seconds. It'll finish quickly. Two legs and a belly still here. Ok, I'll call you after I take my food out of the microwave." Then she hung up.

Either she still thought she had me fooled or thought I was really dumb. Either way, it was painfully obvious she was referring to me being dead in a minute or less after she injected me. The two legs and a belly were her, Humberto and Seth with his big pot belly. Not only was she cunning and sneaky like Gina, she also was not that bright. Intelligence was a trait both Gina and Anita lacked. I was all too familiar with code-languages since Gina shared many code languages with her lovers. She had code names, code meeting places and codes for sex. The thrill of pulling the wool of someone's eyes and scheming turned her on. The code language both spiced things up and kept her from getting caught by her lovers' wives.

In addition to her 10-year beau, she shared codes with Caleb when texting him for intimate moments. "Beer" was their code for sex. She would text him, "I waiting for you to bring me two cold beers and put them in my cooler." It's interesting how her texts came through occasionally while he was lying next to me and I had no idea all those times it was my best friend texting him. She was a sneaky wench. Her code name "Aniger" would appear on his phone. It was her name spelled backward. So thanks to Gina's underhandedness and schooling me on the language of cheating, Anita wasn't able to pull a fast one.

Presumably she was talking to either Landan or Caleb. Landan generally is inaccessible and sleep after

10 p.m., so she was probably on the phone with Caleb. Regardless of who she was talking to, I had enough — enough of her, Seth, Humberto and those on the outside including Landan, Caleb, Brent and Gina. Although Gina's hand wasn't in it per se she played a large part because she was aware of the videotaping, kidnapping and murder plots, and she went along to get me out the picture. To get even, I included her in my plan. I couldn't continue to live in fear and lose sleep. I became vulnerable to their never-ending schemes, plots and lies. Even so, the end didn't seem near — unless I brought it to an end myself.

Since they played these dangerous games for so long, it was now my turn. I decided to dramatize and succumb to the crazy role they planted to gain more time in the hospital. I got up from the chair, paced back and forth down the hall to design a powerful plan. I knew I needed to begin with cancelling my life insurance policy. Connor from Human Resources still hadn't gotten back to me, a half a million dollars was hanging over my head, so I decided to resign first thing in the morning as head scientist of pharmaceutical drug development, effective immediately. The resignation would automatically terminate the coverage. My career was important to me, and I needed the job but also needed the certainty of the policy cancellation. Although it was set to expire the following day, there was a possibility of automatic renewal whether I opted in or not. Frankly, it wasn't worth the risk. I refused to allow my tormentors to win and financially benefit by my demise. If they killed me, so what. They weren't going to get my money. They were scavengers for money, always looking for ways to benefit off someone else, no matter whether they had to cheat, lie or steal to get it.

Had they invested the same amount of energy into themselves professionally, academically or entrepreneurially, they too might have been able to build their own successful, legitimate empire. I always told them they should do more with their lives. They were disgusted, and disappointed with themselves and life's failures. Their only resort was to take it from someone who made it in life.

I lost track of time before I realized the nurses were in the middle of a shift change. I'd been pacing and thinking for hours and hadn't even noticed breakfast was delivered to the unit. Some people had even showered. The treatment team met individually with the patients on the unit. One by one, they were discharged, including the Bonnie and Clyde duo, Seth and Anita. Thank God. While patients waited in the lobby for their escort downstairs, I sat at the dining hall table gazing out the window. Seth limped by in his cast with his brown paper bag filled with his belongings and said I was next to see the doctor. He was confident I was getting discharged as well, figuring they didn't keep patients beyond five days.

He notified Landan and Caleb that I was being released and told them to have the white van waiting outside to snatch me as I left the hospital. Little did he know I'd already met with the doctor. I played the "crazy" card well enough for the shrink to give me three more days. It was the time I needed to quietly devise a master plan. Just like the other times I'd escaped their plots, Seth and Anita looked shocked when I sarcastically waved goodbye as they walked to the secured door to leave.

"Aren't you leaving too, Laila?" Seth asked.

"No, they didn't discharge me. I'm here for another week."

"What? Why?"

"They said I wasn't ready to leave and want to watch over me a few more days. I'm really upset about it because I'm ready to go home."

"Wow, really? I thought just about everyone was being discharged today?"

"It seems almost everyone except me."

Even though I was going to be in the hospital only another three days, Seth didn't need to know that so I told him a week. That would give the assailants four days in the freezing cold to wait outside for me when I'd already gone home. I'd learned from Landan and Caleb that you can't let everyone know your plan and what you're thinking. "Everything ain't for everybody", Caleb often professed. At least I learned a few ways of the street from them, along with their other mantra from the "48 Laws of Power" book, which is what they used as nothing more than a toolbox of mind games and manipulative tactics. The last time I checked knowledge was power, not manipulation.

Seth expected me to walk out the front entrance with them and into their booby trap. Yellow taxi cabs were lined outside to bring the patients home. In my case, they had a personal chauffeur waiting in a white van to whisk me away. That wasn't going to happen. I was glad to see them leave and felt such relief. This was the only time I wasn't startled by the loud slam of unit door, it was music to my ears. For the first time, I slept in my room and had a good night's sleep. With Seth and Anita no longer on the unit, I felt so much better. They were both slimy, slithering snakes.

Humberto was a snake as well. I bumped into him in the hall and assertively told him I was on to him and promised to report him to administration if his nonsense continued. Point blank. He'd been with the hospital 13 years, risked his job and his vested retirement. Of course, he acted like he didn't know what I was talking about. But the expression on his face spoke volumes and assured me he knew. He got the message. I laughed in his face and walked away, shaking my head. "What an idiot," I said to myself. I knew mocking him would further upset him, entice him to seek revenge and have the white van outside waiting on Day Seven. Therefore, to sweeten my plan, I secretly booked a one-way flight to the Florida Keys and arranged for a medic cab to take me to the airport on Day Three.

The shrink and psychiatric nurse who were both

convinced about the plots, notified local authorities of the assailant's names and agreed to help. The nurse arranged to have me lie on a gurney with a toe tag while they called Code Blue. Covered with a white sheet, they transported me to the service elevator and out the back door to the awaiting medic cab. It was the perfect plan and worked like a charm, and I was off to the airport.

florida bound

With so much chaos and confusion in the air, I needed to get away from Charleston for a while and was glad to board the aircraft to Florida. Moving back to Charleston after nine years of living in the City of Brotherly Love was a culture shock and a harsh reality. It was a necessary evil because I was able to see some people for who they really were. From my closest friends, I had endured betrayal, wickedness, and hatred. Their authentic bitter core was revealed and their artificial exterior exposed. Isolation and confusion consumed me. I no longer knew who my true friends were and questioned the authenticity of those around me. The three years I'd been back in Charleston, I was connected to world's most envious and hateful friends who turned into enemies. My infamous frenemies painted smiling faces to mask their hate and malicious intent to deceive those on the outside looking in.

My trusted friend Gina betrayed me. Tabatha and Landan betrayed me. And Caleb — well, Caleb doesn't matter. Easy come, easy go. I would have never imagined at this point in my life, or any point, I would have adversaries like these, if at all. Nor would I have imagined confrontations, dramatic episodes, and plots against me. It must have been the consequence of befriending people with small minds with nothing to lose. I knew long ago they were not equipped to be on my team; they lacked the fundamental pillars of trust, credibility, and respect to produce champions. Either I did an inadequate job at weeding out the riff raff, or they did a great job at pulling the wool over my eyes.

Within the last week, they attempted to secretly roll up on me with plans of using Caleb's spare key to invade my home and attack me. They tracked my whereabouts using a mobile GPS app, created a real-life murder-for-hire plot, and enlisted hospital staff and Landan's close mafia associates from New York City and Charlotte to execute their plan. It was an exhausting journey with one turning event after another. Deceit, jealousy, and greed were their driving force, torment and malice their vehicle. In almost every attempt, they used people I was close to including two other girlfriends, Tamara and Arnell. Tamara and I knew each other for almost 30 years and used to live with me during high school when her mother kicked her out. Arnell and I were also from the same town but became close friends in our latter years. Caleb and Landan used them to entrap me, get reports on me, and to lure me on their turf. But it never worked. They were so desperate in all of their attempts.

In that same time frame before I went into the hospital, Tabatha indirectly mentioned Caleb and Gina planned to create a lie around town in effort to publicly humiliate me. Caleb came up with the defamatory idea that flimsy Gina co-signed since she could have never thought of such a plan herself. In attempts to assassinate my character, they collaborated to label me psychotic, schizophrenic, and emotionally unstable. Tabatha also mentioned they planned to appear to be concerned friends by reaching out to my family and loved ones about their concern for my mental well-being, including a couple unsuspecting family members of mine. I was in such disbelief, and to my surprise, Tabatha divulged the explicit details.

"Listen, I'm just going to tell you. They're up to no good, and I'm in the middle. I love both of you guys, and this is really hard for me. I don't want to see either of you hurt. Caleb is a horrible person and he convinced Gina to say you're crazy and hearing voices," she said.

"Are you kidding me?"

"No, I'm not. They are planning to call your aunts and other family to act like they're so concerned about you and your mental stability. They're going to say you're psychotic and convince them that you need to be institutionalized."

"Is this a joke?"

"Laila, you're a very smart woman, and you'll be able to figure this out. I told Gina she needs to stop dealing with Caleb because he is very dangerous. This is all just bad — a bad dream. I really wish you never met that man. If you hadn't, he wouldn't be in any of our lives. I told her, 'If he's telling you his plans to harm her, imagine what he might do to you?' He can't be trusted."

"Well, first of all, we both know Gina's not the sharpest tool in the toolbox and she'll go along with anything to give herself a makeover and give the illusion of being the best side-chick. But I have to admit, I'm surprised she would go against me like that, especially knowing his harmful intent."

"Yeah, it's horrible," Tabatha agreed.

I discovered they contacted many of my family members and acquaintances to enact their vicious plot. Gina had a childlike voice, an angelic exterior with a soft juvenile tone of innocence. Her gentle, quiet nature was very deceiving. My relatives knew that she and I had been dear friends for 20 years, and only heard me speak great things about her. So when she called my family with her fabricated concern to plant the rumor she helped create, they were inclined to believe her. After all, they had no reason to suspect otherwise. Little did they know she was a conniving liar, two-timing backstabber, and a woman of many faces with multiple dark secrets. She lied to her own family for many years about her secret life, so naturally she would have no hesitation or guilt in lying to mine. She also bore no shame in seeing her sweet mother fervently pray that she would one day marry the man she'd been seeing for 10 years — not knowing he was already married — to someone else.

My family's initial belief in Gina and Caleb's lie disappointed me, yet I understood their rationale. They had been manipulated and sweetly deceived but as I explained to them, if she'd lie to her daughter for 20 years about the true identity of her father, certainly she'd lie to my family. Her younger daughter had doubts and questioned Gina but she continued to mislead her. Gina was good at fooling people, and further fooled her daughter by suggesting a DNA test, knowing her daughter would refuse. Gina feared the paternity test because it would expose her lie of two decades.

No one knew the real Gina. I must admit, her and Caleb's idea was brilliant — to create a damaging lie about someone you're plotting against while simultaneously pretending to be concerned so people wouldn't know you're truly the villain. Pretty clever, and it almost worked until I played the surprise audio recording of my phone conversations with Tabatha disclosing Gina and Caleb's demonic scheme. My family was shocked to hear the recording, and felt growing resentment toward Gina.

I began recording Tabatha's calls because I didn't trust her. She always spoke negatively to us about the other, discussed other folks' private business and gave far too much time to neighborhood gossip. She simply couldn't be trusted. Recording conversations was a regular practice for Tabatha and something she'd often speak of. So I downloaded a recording app to my smartphone and recorded the last week of our calls, just as she did mine.

I hadn't realized so many evil and cold people existed in this world. Charleston had too much drama and crabs-in-a-barrel for me. Getting away was what I needed, especially after Landan increased the bounty for my head. I'd already quit my job, arranged care for Zion, and planned to stay a few months in Florida with my good friend, Bethany.

Beth and her husband, Andrew, invited me to stay with them at their new home in Florida. She and I became friends when we both lived in Nashville some time ago. She was a tall beautiful woman with silky skin and curly brown hair. People were instantly drawn to her gregarious personality and magnetic energy. You could always find her working the room, socializing, and wearing a large smile. You could hear her cackling laugh from across the room. Ironically, we met seven years ago in Tampa while attending the National Association of Pharmaceutical Scientists conference. We immediately clicked and remained friends ever since.

Professionally, socially, and spiritually we were on the same page. We flourished in our careers as scientists, adored our families, and often enjoyed an evening out on the town after a long week on the job in the chemistry lab. We worked for competing pharmaceutical companies and both specialized in drug development. After winning a federal grant, together we designed a drug therapy using synthetic ingredients to treat embryo defects, and we presented a proposal to the Food and Drug Administration for approval of our drug.

We were ambitious, smart, and young, and earned a salary others dreamed of. It was great to finally meet someone with whom I shared so many commonalities and one who wasn't threatened by my success, beauty, or popularity. There was no room for competition or jealousy because we were both successful, wanted more out of life, and didn't settle for mediocrity. Good wasn't good enough for us. Although we were both distinguished research scientists, we also knew how to have a good time. She was so much fun and always made me laugh. We'd always find a reason to raise our wine glasses for a toast.

"Here's to real friendship."

"Here's to the good life."

"... to never settling."

"... to happiness."

"... to us."

"Cheers."

Laughter and the sound of clinking wine glasses followed each salute. Never a dull moment with her. I rarely had this much fun with Gina and Tabatha because they were always stuck up, judgmental, and gossiping. They seldom had money and often needed to wait until their next payday, or borrowed from Peter to pay Paul. I wasn't used to delayed fun. I often questioned my connection with them since we shared absolutely nothing in common and never had meaningful or valuable dialogue. This was the real reason why Gina was often quiet — not because she was shy but because she wasn't able to articulate an intellectual conversation. These women lacked everything I stood for. Their negative energy was exhausting, their values were distorted, and their integrity was nonexistent.

The flight to Florida was just over three hours with a brief stop in Atlanta. Once we landed, the beautiful sunshine, majestic palm trees, and white sandy beaches welcomed me. Florida greeted me with gracious hospitality and a kiss from the illuminating sun. Immediately, I experienced joy and was filled with warmth. Retreating to Florida was long overdue. Beth understood I had endured a lot and wanted me to relax and not think about the past. To distract me from the craziness, she arranged for us to stay three days at her in-law's eight-bedroom beach house directly facing the Gulf of Mexico. The place was breathtaking. The 1876 historic home had 20-foot vaulted ceilings, furnishings imported from Peru, an indoor heated pool, and a magnificent theater room. We felt like royalty in the oversized estate supplied with a uniformed house staff of six, an Italian-speaking chef, and three private balconies with unobstructed panoramic views of the emerald-green coast.

Once we walked through the tall vintage French doors, we entered the world of the rich and famous. Two champagne glasses and a bottle of Dom Perignon White Gold Jeroboam garnished with ruby-red strawberries awaited us, compliments of her wealthy in-laws. The imported French sparkling wine was so magnificent and smooth with a marvelous taste of luxury in every sip. Outside were two blue-canopied cabanas on the private beach, one for each of us. I could have lain there forever as I enjoyed the radiance of the illuminating sun on my arms and legs.

Beth and I hadn't seen each other in a couple of years and spent the next few hours catching up while enjoying champagne. No matter how long we had been apart, it always seemed like yesterday. We rhythmically picked up where we left off. With the comfort of the cabanas and the caressing of the sun combined with my second glass of champagne, I was so relaxed and couldn't stop yawning. Before long, I was fast asleep. Beth left me to rest a couple hours and woke me up at the request of the house staff to freshen up for dinner. The chef prepared a magnificent meal influenced by a fusion of Southern, Latin American and Italian cultures. His signature key lime pie was served for dessert. The amazing beach house, staff, and breathtaking views made me want to call the movers to pack my things in Charleston and ship them to Florida.

Florida was peaceful, serene, and liberating. Surrounded by endless nature and God's creation, I was completely free from weariness, anxiousness, and stress. I was in a new space and embraced the tranquility of the splashing waves. Just before dusk, Beth and I took a stroll along Panama City's white sandy beach. We walked closer to shore with our bare feet immersed in the cool sand. Just before approaching the wooden dock, we stopped to impulsively inscribe our names in the sand with our fingertips, and laughed at our silliness as we watched the waves wash our masterpieces away. We walked on the long dock and sat at the very end that stretched 200 feet into the endless ocean. Our feet dangled over the edge as we stared across the gulf and watched the radiant red sun slowly disappear below the horizon.

mimosas on a silver platter

Our weekend in Panama City Beach was amazing and went by extremely fast. It was everything I went there for — relaxation, peace of mind, and 27 miles of the crystal white sandy beach. Each morning we were awakened to the soft sound of splashing waves, the smell of pecan-cinnamon rolls, and the beauty of daybreak. I could have stayed in Panama City forever, but Beth needed to return home to prepare for work the following day. The house staff greeted us with a vintage silver platter in one hand serving crystal stem flute glasses filled with pineapple mimosas and floating strawberries. We enjoyed breakfast on the oversized bedroom balcony overlooking the east end of the gulf before our two-hour drive to Beth's. Our luggage was pre-loaded in her new luxury sedan, and a small-handle basket filled with assorted snacks and fruit were placed on the front seat by the house staff.

Every turn on the scenic highway was breathtaking. The drive had picturesque views of clear blue skies, turquoise water and trees as far as the eye could see. Several free-spirited tourists chased high-flying kites along the bay. The open space and fresh January breeze made a perfect day for those interested in the growing sport. The enjoyment of running through the breeze validated they were in a fun, care-free space.

As we drove down Florida's panhandle, my feet were propped over the glove box and my seat was slightly reclined. The rushing wind blew through the window as Beth accelerated onto the freeway. We talked, laughed and sang the entire 105 miles to her new house. Before long, we pulled into her half-moon driveway paved with pink and gray marble stones. Palm trees cascaded over the driveway and manicured front lawn. Once inside, I was blown away. The one-story house was 2,300 square feet with many twists, turns and endless design details. The open gourmet kitchen overlooked the sunken great room with built-in bookcases, a gigantic flat screen television and wall-to-wall collapsing sliding glass doors leading to an L-shaped screened patio with a bar, two ceiling fans, two patio furniture sets and an upgraded outdoor kitchenette. Beth was too afraid for us to enjoy the patio since she saw a curly tailed gecko crawling under the patio table last summer.

Her home was as tranquil as the beachfront estate in Panama City. The only thing missing was the amazing house staff and majestic views of the emerald coast, but this place had the peace I needed after the tormenting in Charleston. Her back yard faced a large man-made lake surrounded by a dozen estate homes. The lake hosted beautiful decks, exotic fish, and paddle boats. An elegant fountain propelling nine feet of spraying water was centered in the lake. While she and her husband, Andrew, unloaded our things from the car, I sat on the patio enjoying the peaceful view. Nature's outdoor offered a quiet calmness that allowed me to have empty thoughts about nothing. Sitting on the patio chair, I took a deep breath, relaxed my shoulders, and wished life could continue to be this good when I returned home. As much as I was prepared to start all over in Florida, I knew I couldn't live my life in fear, always watching my back or running from suspected troublemakers so eventually I would have to return to the wilderness.

Beth came out to the patio with her arm stretched out with my cell phone.

"Here, Laila, your phone keeps going off."

"Thanks, you didn't have to bring it out here."

"It's all good, no worries."

"It was my email alert. I have a ton of new messages. Wait! Why did Caleb send me an email? I can only imagine what he has to say."

"Oh my goodness, girl, what does he want? You should just delete it and not even bother to read it. Screw him," she said as she waved her hand to dismiss his email.

"I'm going to read it. He probably just has a bunch of lies to tell."

---------- Original message ----------

From: Caleb McElroy <thejuiceman@live.net>

Date: Mon, Jan 13, 2014 at 3:45 pm

Subject: vacation

To: Laila Roberts <l.roberts@aol.com>

I heard you were on vacation, and wanted to say hello and have a nice time. I'm sorry things turned out the way they did and I never meant to hurt you. I've had you on my mind a lot lately and truly miss you. I even called your brother about you this morning.

Enjoy your trip!

C

---------- Reply message ----------

From: Laila Roberts <l.roberts@aol.com>

Date: Mon, Jan 13, 2014 at 3:57 pm

Subject: RE: vacation

To: Caleb McElroy <thejuiceman@live.net>

Good afternoon. Please don't call my brother about me. I'm not associated with you, Gina, or any such foolishness. I am not thinking about you. I've been on the sunny beaches of Florida along the Gulf of Mexico, had an amazing impromptu & needed vacation. I'm sure you are missing me since Gina and I are NOTHING alike. I would miss me too. It is what is, and this email is wasted energy, or at least it is for me. Fake people were exposed and removed from life. That's a blessing in of itself!! I have surrounded myself with Eagles so I can continue to fly high, and to continue to give people a reason to hate on me! I'm on to bigger things! Many blessings & God bless!

---------- Reply message ----------

From: Caleb McElroy <thejuiceman@live.net>

Date: Mon, Jan 13, 2014 at 4:03 pm

Subject: vacation

To: Laila Roberts l.roberts@aol.com

Ok cool... I'm sorry you feel that way. No need for a response. I won't contact you again, and don't contact me with your foolishness!!

---------- Reply message ----------

From: Laila Roberts <l.roberts@aol.com>

Date: Mon, Jan 13, 2014 at 4:17 pm

Subject: RE: vacation

To: Caleb McElroy <thejuiceman@live.net>

Foolishness?! Now, Isn't that the pot calling the kettle black. You two are a great example of ... wait, I won't judge. And please ... don't inquire to your cousin about me either. She told me last week when I got out the hospital. Our names should never come out of each other's mouths. Like I said, as always, I'm on to much bigger things. Some people can't & won't soar this high -- and living in someone's shadow & riding coat tails won't help. YES, I know friends are envious of me -- why else would a friend want a man I was dating -- past, present or future? She did me a favor by fooling around with you because it killed two birds with one stone. When people ask me about her, which they will, now and 10 years from now, they'll know the truth of why we're no longer friends. Farewell, goodbye, so long!! It's certainly a HAPPY NEW YEAR!! Take care .... God bless!

All smiles :-) ... See you at the top!

----------- Original message ----------

From: Caleb McElroy <thejuiceman@live.net>

Date: Mon, Jan 13, 2014 at 4:35 pm

Subject: vacation

To: Laila Roberts <l.roberts@aol.com>

Yeah... What da phuck ever!!! Chile please ... inquiring about you thru my cousin??? I'll wait for your answer ...You've gotta be kidding me!!! Lmfaooo ... No, Hunny ... I was not!!!

Now why would I go and do a thing like that, when I feel as though weight has been lifted off my chest???

Oh... and if we do meet at the top...

Act like you don't know me...

---------- Reply message ----------

From: Laila Roberts <l.roberts@aol.com>

Date: Mon, Jan 13, 2014 at 4:47 pm

Subject: RE: vacation

To: Caleb McElroy <thejuiceman@live.net>

Perhaps I misread her text; I pasted a screenshot of her text below. I didn't think you would have a reason to inquire, just as you would have no reason to call my brother this morning. It's all good. By the way, you don't have to worry about me acting like I don't know you if I see you at the top. Respectfully, you two are irrelevant & nonexistent to me. I have no desire to acknowledge either of you -- at the top, or any level -- although "you" are more likely to get to the top through the advancement of someone else. But if you do make it, I'll be so emerged into my own success that I won't see either of you coming or going. Take care. No reply needed.

---------- Original message ----------

From: Caleb McElroy <thejuiceman@live.net>

Date: Mon, Jan 13, 2014 at 4:52 pm

Subject: vacation

To: Laila Roberts <l.roberts@aol.com>

Don't tell me I don't need to reply. And what is this "you two" shit you speak of??? Ain't nobody touch ya lil pint-size, dwarf-looking, ugly friend. I told you, she's not my type. If you feel so strongly about it, why don't you kick her ass, it might make you feel better?

---------- Reply message ----------

From: Laila Roberts <l.roberts@aol.com>

Date: Mon, Jan 13, 2014 at 5:02 pm

Subject: RE: vacation

To: Caleb McElroy <thejuiceman@live.net>

We're both intelligent so let's speak as such. I stooped to lower-level conversations since I've been back in Charleston, and accommodated the intellectual deficiencies of others. Although I can communicate from the po'-house to the White House, it gets boring after a while.

And by the way, weight lifted off your chest? Yes, I rode you because I don't cooperate with nonsense or in sharing a man -- especially a man my friend is seeing. You're better off in her defiled bed because she's cooperative and puts up with the mess that I simply will not deal with. She revealed her greatest assets with short skirts and low scissor-cut shirts so no need to learn what she's thinking because after all, you are not sleeping with her for her mind. I'm confident in who I am, and not interested in "just having fun"! For some, I'm difficult, intimidating, and more than what they deserve. So yes ... I'm sure it's weight lifted. Sometimes the "easy" route is best. Your opinion of me does not define me and does not matter. Like I said, I don't see people coming or going. Enjoy the remainder of your day. And please don't reply this time!

* * *

I had enough of going back and forth with Caleb. As with anything else with him, it was all lies and pointless dialogue. Nothing ever comes from these types of exchanges with him except headaches and drained energy. Further, why would a nearly 50-year-old man suggest I have a physical altercation with someone, let alone a former close friend? I am not in favor of violence or conducting myself on that level. As it turned out, he wanted to create further conflict between Gina and me to maximize the distraction while he and other clandestine individuals carried out their ambitious plot.

This was a classic example of what I didn't want to return home to. I was certain the never-ending saga of Caleb and the tormentors would continue. Prior to reading his emails, I was in a relaxed space and had such peace of mind. Within minutes, the acid exchange had brought in the Charleston storm and vacuumed my joy. I should have listened to Beth and deleted his emails without ever reading them. I would have saved myself from the turmoil, lies, and provocation.

I returned to the family room and stretched out on the spacious sectional sofa filled with decorative fluffy pillows and my propped my head on them. Two more antagonizing emails came in from Caleb. This time I refused to read them and simply clicked on the delete key from my phone. I needed to just relax, close my eyes and hear the peaceful sound of the outdoors through the opened sliding doors. Beth and her husband were on the opposite side of the house from me. With so much silence and distance between us, you barely knew we were under the same roof. Before we started our plans to cook dinner together, I needed at least an hour of rest.

back to the drama

After two weeks of relaxation in Northern Florida, I prepared to head back to Charleston. Initially I intended to stay another week or two, but my son wanted me to shorten my trip. Zion and I hadn't spent this much time apart, and he really missed his mom. I wanted to get home to him just as much and sleep again in my own bed. No matter how spectacular the trip, nothing felt as good as that. The past two weeks had been amazing. Beth and her husband helped take things off my troubled mind.

Their warmth and authenticity reminded me of the beauty of good friendships, loving souls, and true Southern hospitality. I couldn't have asked for a better trip or better friends. Each night we enjoyed each other's company and reminisced over a home-cooked meal and glasses of crisp white wine. To show my appreciation, I prepared a delightful dinner each night before they came home from work.

We laughed about the good times we had in Atlanta when we regularly visited from Nashville. We giggled ourselves to tears thinking about all the fun. We were a little bit younger then, enjoyed the nightlife, and could hang until the early morning hours. Spontaneously, we decided to take a drive to Atlanta for a few days. The following morning we were on the road headed up I-75. Similar to our drive along Florida's panhandle, our drive through South Georgia was just as relaxing. It was a little less scenic but soothing nonetheless. Some of the towns were so small we passed through them in the blink of an eye. Other towns looked depressed with boarded-up stores, faulty gas stations, and weary-looked workers with heavy Southern accents. We passed by weed-strewn lots, deserted peach orchards, and peanut fields. South Georgia has a rich history filled with many historic sites, landmarks, and monuments. A few times Beth and I oohed and ahhed and thought of stopping, but we were more interested in getting to our stomping grounds in Atlanta before I flew back to Charleston.

In Atlanta, we stayed in the residential-style suites at the W Hotel in Atlanta's affluent midtown area. Our 33rd-floor balcony had panoramic views of the city's beautiful skyline and magnificent views of Stone Mountain Park. Years ago, when Beth and I lived in Nashville, we came to Atlanta often so this felt like our home away from home. We had a chance to see close friends, dine at our favorite restaurants, and max out our credit cards at the swank clothing and shoe boutiques. We loved those shops because we could always find original pieces that were not sold in regular retail chain stores. Atlanta and Florida both offered the lifestyle and enjoyment Beth and I were accustomed to. We were no longer interested in the happening social scene so we enjoyed a few new jazz and cigar lounges. The concierge was kind enough to give us two complimentary tickets to the nearby comedy show with valet service. We had such a great time that the last two nights in town, we stayed in and simple enjoyed each other's company. The ripping and running caught up with us, so we rented old classics on the hotel's movie channel, got a couple of bottles of wine, and slumbered in our double comfortable beds.

Several times during our Atlanta trip I received text messages from so-called friends wanting to know when I was coming back home. The texts were so random without a greeting, I knew their messages were influenced by Caleb and Landan. One of the one women, Tamara, who messaged me wasn't aware that I knew she had a connection with Caleb. Some things everyone doesn't need to know and I never said a word.

Her text read, "Hey girl, when are you coming back?"

I looked down at my phone to read the text, shook my head, and waited a while to reply. A courtesy hello would have been nice, so I was in no rush to send my "I have no idea" response. Besides, she only asked so she could report my return to Caleb.

"Well, just come back in time for the annual gala."

"Absolutely," I replied, although the gala was the farthest thing from my mind and so was she. I was not interested in returning to Charleston to continue to deal with the phony people. Their insincerity and cold nature reminded me of the abrupt hardness of those I knew from New York. Fast-paced people brusquely bumping into each other with no apology, the sharpness of their tongues, and their cutthroat schemes qualities I couldn't handle. It's the same attitude I wanted to stay far away from. I decided to spend less time with friends, more time with Zion. I also needed to catch up on the many things I neglected while dating Caleb. The unhealthy relationship had been a horrible distraction from my priorities and completely threw me off balance. That should have been a warning sign, but I was blinded by the perception of love and continued on the turbulent emotional ride.

After two days of rest, Beth drove me to the airport. We had a teary-eyed goodbye at the north side of Atlanta's busy airport. I didn't want the vacation to end, but I grabbed the long handle on my luggage and wheeled it toward the seemingly interminable lines. As I moved closer to the security screening check point, an old friend working as a TSA agent noticed me and advanced me to the front of the line. His hand gesture was graceful and unnoticeable to not cause an uproar with the impatiently waiting travelers. Before long I boarded the air-conditioned winter flight. Thank God I dressed in layers because it could have been an uncomfortable, frigid trip. The flight attendants made sure we were all seated and prepared for departure. They gave their scripted instructions on seat belts, floatation devices, and ceiling-dropping oxygen masks.

"When the seat belt sign illuminates, you must fasten your seat belt. In the event of a decompression, an oxygen mask will automatically appear in front of you. To start the flow of oxygen, pull the mask toward you", she instructed as she pointed her hand to the emergency exits to give the next instruction.

The airline really should give headsets with pre-recorded instructions to the inexperienced travelers so the experienced passengers do not have to hear the repetitive instruction over and over. The nonstop Delta flight to Charleston was one hour and 10 minutes. I was glad to be back home and looked forward to seeing my son. I didn't tell anyone about my return and planned to remain low key for a few days before calling anyone. My last two weeks had been so peaceful and serene that I wanted the days ahead to be the same without the constant buzz from my vibrating cell phone. Returning home felt foreign with a deep awkward silence. In Florida, the silence was of peace and tranquility but this silence was of emptiness. Something intangible was terribly missing. The free-spirited people, laughter, and joy were gone. The absence of the radiant sun made it appear gloomy and grey. It was very different from the clear blue skies and emerald green waters in Panama City and the welcoming warmth of Atlanta.

Aside from dreary weather, it was nice to spend quality time with Zion again. We watched his favorite shows, played board games, and just enjoyed family time in the house. Then, after a month of being home, the luring phone calls and Facebook messages from artificial friends began to trickle in, especially from my other close friends Arnell and Tamara. They weren't aware I knew they were part of the scheme to get closer to me to find out what was going on in my life but I played along. I hadn't received so many invites to social events, outings, and all-expense paid vacations before. The irony is that these were invitations to vulnerability and isolation to enable Landan, Caleb, and their accomplices to carry out their plot.

If they had invested the same amount of energy into themselves, they would not have been compelled to plot to take wealth from someone else, and could have used that same energy to create their own brand and wealth. Close friends monitored and reported my whereabouts, stalked my home, and devised a plan of attack. They recruited people close to me, bullied my family, and promised attractive incentives to others to manipulate my trust. It wasn't hard to separate the real from the fake. More and more people were tipping the scale with fakeness. Some I just cut off while others I kept around to make them believe they were fooling me. But after a while, it grew old, and I grew tired of the deception, indirect harassment and phony friends around me.

I hoped the attempts would stop, but the calls and inbox messages from synthetic mutual friends confirmed it would surely continue. I knew it had to do with the insurance policy Landan and Caleb got wind of. Although I modified the policy and terminated Gina as the executor and trustee, I contacted an estate attorney to revise the document once again. This time, I didn't tell anyone, not even my family. I made surprising changes to the will and hired the lawyer's firm to manage the estate and trust. I also appropriated just enough funds in trust to cover the cost of Zion's college and related expenses, payable directly the institution. I willed the remainder to charity, listing three of my alma maters as recipients. I deemed it to be the appropriate and responsible thing to do. I wanted a scholarship created in my name or a library erected in my honor, so hopefully through these gifts my dreams would be realized.

I couldn't believe immediately following the change, Landan recruited several more of his associates to stalk and torment me. They followed me to the Piccadilly for brunch after church. A couple of them were seated in the restaurant pretending to order a meal but only to keep an eye on me. Two of the men were actual family friends, and two others were close friends of Landan's. I knew something wasn't right the moment I walked to the lobby register to pay for my meal. Two additional rough-looking men, one of whom was definitely Landan's friend, approached me on both sides and slowly moved closer to corner me once I walked out the restaurant. Their suspicious and abnormal behavior was painfully obvious and warranted alarm. What they had in mind was unknown, but I knew it wasn't going to include me, so I called the local authorities using my alternative cell phone. Since they had successfully intercepted phone towers, I purchased a second mobile phone connected to a completely different tower with a completely new area code, although Arnell later disclosed this confidential information to Landan.

To devise a demonic plan on a holy day or any day you had to be a cruel and heartless person. Enough was enough. Once the police officers arrived in two separate patrol cars, I walked outside the restaurant to give them the description of the suspects inside. I noticed four more of Landan's friends outside waiting in three different SUV's alongside of the restaurant. Another sat outside the restaurant's door on the wooden bench. Considering it was only 17 degrees out, it seemed a bit unusual to sit outside in the freezing cold for an extended period. I told the officers about the two suspects inside lurking behind me. "All these recruits to monitor and capture one person?"

Every time I took a step so did they. I purposely turned in a different direction to see if they would persist in following, and to no surprise, they did. Two additional times I subtly faked a move and they were close on my tail. I thought their behavior constituted grounds for stalking and aggravated harassment charges. But since they hadn't verbally approached me there wasn't anything legally the police could do other than document the events. Instead, they escorted me to their nearby station to safety as the tormenters watched me drive away.

sunday brunch

Never would I have imagined this type of drama as part of my world. The day began beautifully with crisp Winter skies but ended horribly. I didn't feel like getting out of my Queen Anne vintage bed or going to morning service. I had a long enjoyable night, stayed over my girlfriend's house and didn't necessarily want to drive all the way home to Mt. Pleasant to get myself together and drive all the way back to Charleston for church. My plans were to simply go home, relax, and watch Joel Osteen on the Christian Network channel.

As with every Sunday, my cousin Olivia called me on FaceTime to see if I was up preparing for church. Our weekly custom was to meet each Sunday at church for the early sunrise service, sit together in the center pew, and go for brunch following service. This was our cousin-bonding-time. Regardless of how groggy or lazy I felt, her early Sunday morning calls motivated me to get moving. I didn't expect her to call me as early as she did.

"Good morning, Sunshine, how are you?" I answered as I looked at her with her green and red scarf wrapped around her head through the video-conferencing feature on my smartphone.

"I'm good, Laila. It doesn't look like you are up getting ready for church."

"Not at all, but I'm about to pull myself out of bed. I really didn't feel like going this morning. I'm in Charleston and don't feel like driving home to Mt. Pleasant and back to Charleston. I also don't want to miss church, so I'll shower at your place since I'm already on your side of town."

"Well, what time are you coming because I need to pick my friend Sheryl up for church also?"

"I was planning to come in the next few minutes. Is that OK?"

"Well, hurry up and come on."

"OK. To make it easier, I'll pick her up for you. I'm right around the corner from her now, as long as she doesn't mind me picking her up early?"

"Awesome, that'll work. I'll give her a call to tell her that you'll pick her up."

"Great. Let her know I'll be there in 20 minutes."

Sheryl is a sweet older woman with salt-and-pepper hair, and a youthful spirit, gentle heart and warm soul. I never understood how she and Olivia became friends because they are complete opposites. Olivia has a nasty attitude and is bluntly rude to her friends. I guess I could have asked myself the same question about being friends with Tabatha because her attitude was similar to Olivia's, if not worse. Sheryl and I always had great conversation, and sensed she's great company and someone I could learn a lot from. I picked her up since I was nearby. We chatted and laughed during our less than 15-minute drive to church.

"Sheryl, I'm going to let you out here. I'll meet you and Olivia inside church once I get dressed."

"All right, girl. Don't take too long because you're always late."

"I know, I shouldn't be too long. It wouldn't make any sense for me to be as late as I always am considering I'm just around the corner."

Once showered and casually dressed, I finally made it to the historic Georgian-style steeple church with landscaped Spanish moss trees in front. I was late as usual and walked in just before the pastor approached the carpeted pulpit to address the 700 parishioners. Church started at 8 a.m., and I walked in around 9:05 a.m. I definitely need to work on my time management and try getting to church much earlier. I already missed Praise and Worship, Altar Prayer and my good friend's solo performance of his Grammy-nominated Gospel song from his newly released CD. I felt bad because I really wanted to hear him sing and missed his debut on the Grammy's the other night. However, I was just in time for Offering and the

Sermon. Pastor was just getting ready to crack one of his jokes before preparing for Offering.

The Sermons always touched my spirit. Today was no exception. It seemed that Pastor was preaching directly to me today. I felt someone told him what I was going through because everything he said applied to my current stressful situation. He preached about making your haters your motivators, and referenced Psalm 56 when he discussed how your enemies will plot against you, follow you, and wait for you like a roaring lion. He read:

> Be merciful to me, my God,
> for my enemies are in hot pursuit;
> all day long they press their attack.
> [2] My adversaries pursue me all day long;
> in their pride many are attacking me.
> [3] When I am afraid, I put my trust in you.
> [4] In God, whose word I praise —
> in God I trust and am not afraid.
> What can mere mortals do to me?
> [5] All day long they twist my words;
> all their schemes are for my ruin.
> [6] They conspire, they lurk,
> they watch my steps,
> hoping to take my life.
> [7] Because of their wickedness do not let them escape;
> in your anger, God, bring the nations down.

"That was a powerful service, I didn't want service to end," I said to Olivia. "God surely was speaking to me today. Everything he said was relevant to my life."

"Pastor really preached. So what are your plans for the rest of the day?"

"No plan as of yet. I'm probably just going to chill and relax at home."

"You wanna go to brunch?"

"You know I'm always down to eat. Where you wanna go?"

"How about the Piccadilly again?"

"Let's do it. You can ride with me so you don't have to warm your car."

"Perfect, let me see if Sheryl wants to come with us or if we need to bring her home before we go."

The Piccadilly is a well-known Southern cafeteria-style restaurant, and the place many people went to after church on Sunday. Every Sunday Olivia and I went out for breakfast after church, and each Sunday we contemplated where we were going to eat and always ended up at the Piccadilly. We often said we needed to try someplace new, but the Piccadilly was tried and true, and nothing beats their Southern fried catfish, cheese grits and fried green tomatoes.

We weren't able to get our usual table because Sheryl invited her two cousins who also attended church to go with us. They were running about 10 minutes behind, so we waited to order our meal until they arrived.

Similar to each time, Olivia found something to complain about. This time she complained the waitress put the lemon slices in her glass of ice water as opposed to on a side dish. She said the staff doesn't thoroughly wash the lemons before slicing them and the unseen residue and pesticides contaminates her drink. I wouldn't have had an issue with her complaining or letting them know her preferences. It was the manner in which she did it. Her approach was so cold, abrasive and embarrassing. I kept saying I was not going out to eat with her any more, but I never stuck to it.

"Really, Olivia, who complains about that? Good Lord."

"Well, I know how I want my water, and I don't want them dropping those nasty lemons in my water. I asked for them on the side, and that's what I want."

"Well all-righty then."

I was hungry as hell and ready to order. Finally, Sheryl's cousins arrived. One of them you could tell was very sophisticated. She was dressed like a diva with a long fur coat, matching fur hat, and black leather gloves with fur around the trim. She spoke very proper and commanded the attention of the other customers. The only thing missing was her long-stemmed cigarette. The other cousin was a pediatric RN dressed in scrubs, she was just off work from the evening shift, and went straight to church in her Looney Tunes uniform.

"Hey Sheryl, glad you guys were able to make it," I said.

"We would have been here earlier but traffic was crazy. These two ladies are my cousins from Tallahassee."

"Hi there, nice to meet you. Where in Tallahassee do you live?

"You're familiar with Tallahassee?"

"Yes, my girlfriend lives there, not too far from FAMU. I was just down there."

"Wow, really? I'm not that far from FAMU either."

"Small world."

We chit-chatted about Tallahassee, area colleges and the culture of the South compared to the North when I lived in Philly. I always love to talk to Southerners about Southern traditions and Southern charm. During our conversation, I couldn't help notice from the corner of my eye a young man in his mid-20's dining with his lady two tables in front of me. I caught him glancing over at me a few times, and each time we made awkward eye contact.

Why is this man staring at me while his with his girlfriend? I asked myself. I thought it was a little odd the way he would sneak glances at me, and turn his head each time our eyes met.

Sheryl's cousins and I laughed the entire time during breakfast. It was really nice to talk to sweet Southern belles. Olivia, of course, chimed in with negativity and complaints. Brunch was fabulous. I'm not sure about them, but I was ready for a nap.

"Ladies, I'm going to go up front to pay for my check and use the restroom. I'll wait for you up front."

"Ok, Laila. We'll be right out."

As soon as I walked to the cashier to pay for my bill, two men were lurking around in the lobby, both with their eyes glued on me. I recognized one of them as Landan's friend. I saw him many times around Landan and recalled them playing chess together on the hood of a car last summer at the waterfront park on the other side of Charleston. I never forget a face. The man continuously watched me, stared at me, and shadowed my movements. Every time I moved around in the lobby, they moved in the same direction as me. It was not difficult to spot his accomplice because they both looked like he was planning an organized attack. I purposely took a few steps to the left to see if he was going to follow, and he did just as I suspected. His nervous behavior, body language, and appearance were too obvious to ignore. He tried to minimize the visibility of his presence and behavior, but it created another set of suspicions.

Secondly, both men looked out of place. Neither

dined in the restaurant, nor were they paying for a check or making a purchase. They both stood with their eyes glued on me while the other patrons were very engaged in conversation, looking at gifts in the gift shop, or paying for their check. I watched enough espionage shows and Secret Service documentaries on the History channel to know expected behaviors in the natural environment of a restaurant or any other setting for that matter. They simply didn't fit in. The two men weren't doing any of the obvious things one should do in a restaurant, which made their behavior stand out. Their trail on me didn't help my suspicion. I took a moment to process this to make sure I wasn't overthinking or over-reacting, but when something doesn't appear right it usually isn't unless proven otherwise.

Both men had distinctive facial features. Landan's friend had a long scar across his left cheek, and his accomplice was very rough looking with an unshaven face and piercing blue eyes. Both looked like they were preparing to commit a crime or rob a bank. I watched them closely to get a better description. Once they noticed me watching, they walked to the cashier's counter to act as if they were ordering an orange soda pop in a vintage glass bottle. This was deja vu because the same thing occurred at the Super Food Mart when a few teenagers followed me. I quickly paid for my check, looked at the two men and walked back inside the dining area of the restaurant to tell Olivia about the two men.

"Olivia, these two guys out front are following

me."

"What guys? I do not have time for your shit today."

"Oh my God! What are you talking about?"

"I'm not for this today. Who is following you?"

"Come on, walk to the lobby area with me. You see those two guys right there?

"Yes"

"What is that guy's name with the scar?"

"That is LJ's friend's younger brother."

"Yeah, I figured that because they look a lot alike."

"Well, he's in line waiting to be seated, so come on, let's go."

"That's just a front since he knows I'm on to them."

"Well, I'm leaving. I'll catch a ride with Sheryl's cousin. You coming or not? They are not following you."

"OK, leave, but I'm calling the police."

"Why are you calling the cops? Don't call the cops."

Olivia followed behind me to stop me, but whenever my gut tells me something isn't right, that's what I go with and I don't question my instincts. Besides, after Pastor's Sermon earlier, I took heed to my instincts. As I walked back to the cashier's area, the two men continued to follow me. They thought I was walking out of the restaurant. I quietly walked to the back of the foyer and pulled out my second cell phone and called 911.

"911, what is your emergency?"

"Hello sir, my name is Laila Roberts, and two men have tracked to the Piccadilly in North Charleston."

"What do you mean they tracked you?"

"There is a GPS tracker on my car, and they tracked me here."

"Do you know who they are?"

"I don't personally know them, but I have seen them around."

"What are they wearing?"

"Both have on a winter green hoodie."

"Both are wearing winter green hooded sweatshirts?"

"Yes."

"What kind of pants and shoes are they wearing?"

"The black male has on blue jeans with construction boots, and the white male has black painter-style paints and white-leather tennis shoes."

"What are they doing now?"

"They're both now waiting in line pretending to be seated because they know I'm on the phone with the police."

"Did they say anything to you?"

"No they didn't say anything. Their look and body language said it all. They were both watching me, lurking behind me, and closing in on me. Like I said, they were not seated in the restaurant, neither of them ate here this morning, and they weren't out front paying for their check."

"Where are you in the restaurant?"

"I'm in the back of the foyer near the gumball machines waiting in the corner."

"Go toward the door, but do not go outside. You should see two black and white police cars pull up. Do you see them?"

"No, not yet."

"OK, give them a few more seconds. They should be pulling up now. Do you see them?"

"Yes, I see them now."

"OK, Ms. Roberts. The two officers will take it from here. Go ahead and walk outside. I'll stay on the phone until you are near the officers."

I explained the same story to the two responding officers. The two suspicious guys inside, along with two other couples inside monitoring me. All of them were friends of Landan's. I've known Landan for over 25 years, this is what he does and is aligned with his ruthless character.

While standing outside in the frigid cold, in front of the restaurant, the two officers asked several routine questions. By then, I was used to the questions because this is not the first time I was followed or tracked down. The two officers suggested I park my car at their police station overnight until I was able to have it inspected by a mechanic the following day. They escorted me out of the parking lot to head to their station. The police officers noticed two black extended SUV's off to the side of the parking lot approaching my car. One of the drivers I recognized as the guy sitting at the table in front of me with his girlfriend. No wonder they didn't have food at their table. They were sitting there watching me like idiots.

The drivers in the SUVs were unaware the police were escorting me and waited for the police to pull off. The officers gestured for them to drive off. The driver from the restaurant was hesitant and tried to get the police to go ahead of them. The police later told me they suspected they were waiting to follow me and to get them to move on, they shouted through their bullhorn for the drivers to go. The suspects had a look of disgust on their faces and appeared disappointed that I, once again, escaped their plot.

The following morning, I got a ride from a good friend to the police station to get my car. I couldn't trust anyone to bring me so I called a family friend. We drove up the street to the nearby mechanic to have him inspect my car to see if he could locate the GPS tracking device. I was hopeful he wouldn't find one. He said if a GPS device was on my car it would either be electrically wired to the battery so it wouldn't lose its charge, or it would be manually placed underneath the car and someone would have to regularly take it off to charge it. When he looked underneath the dashboard, he located a small black tracker wired to the battery. Although the mechanic was shocked, I was not surprised. I knew a couple of people this was done to and their purpose of tracking them was not to bring them roses.

Now more than ever, I was furious not only because Olivia left me at the Piccadilly but because I knew the borderline geniuses Landan, Caleb, and Brent were responsible for this. Although I had no way to prove it to the police, I knew just how to hold them responsible if something were to happen to me.

over my dead body

I'd had enough of the stalking and the third-party harassment. The assailants knew enough about the penal code to keep themselves out of trouble while continuously pursuing and terrorizing me. They planted rumors from their frivolous story of me having mental issues so if I went to the police for help the cops would think something was psychologically wrong. Indeed it was a brilliant plan, but it also showed me who the weakest-links and true supporters were.

Those who erred on their side I cut off. I have the gift of goodbye and could cut a person off as if I never knew them. It gave me great pleasure to see those same individuals later return with tearful apologies. The assailants knew my routine, knew I am my mother's only child and that the two strongest male figures in my life were recently deceased. They assumed I had no one to turn to for help and used that as their way to try to isolate me. They bullied, manipulated, and even recruited some of the men in my family all for a buck which I made sure none of them would ever see. Even though my family disliked Landan, he used Tabatha to lie to them to get them unknowingly on his side by employing another one of his adopted philosophies, "Learn how to use enemies". All of this was getting old as they continued to haunt me, and throw verbal stones at my character and reputation. There is definite truth in the phrase "Never throw stones at a woman with grenades." It was only a matter of time before I exploded. I needed to take matters into my own hands and settle this myself once and for all. I had to put an end to them myself. I'd been around them long enough to learn their philosophy of "stop the enemy," which meant completely get rid of the enemy by any means necessary. In all of their scheming and studying of the "48 Laws of Power," they overlooked one important detail, "Know who you're dealing with and never upset the wrong person."

To prepare for war, I enrolled into a local gun safety course. The training was required by the state to apply for a license to carry a firearm. I could have easily purchased a weapon from one of Landan's or Caleb's troubled friends but I needed to obtain my weapon the legal way. I figured since they initiated the rumor of me being schizophrenic, I could use insanity as a defense and not inherit criminal charges for possession or discharge of a loaded firearm or any other related charges. So the voices in my head they rumored I was having, were telling me to kill. It's ironic how the tables turned. Their slander and malice would work in my favor should I ever need to use my weapon on them. It was a classic case of poetic justice. As

Confucius professed, "Before you embark on a journey of revenge, dig two graves." One for me, and one for you. The very plot you set for me, God may turn and set for you. I sincerely hoped they returned to my home so I could greet them with their own element of surprise because my door is locked for their protection, not mine. This time, their only way out is in a tailor-made body bag.

The certified course instructor was a retired FBI agent and trained sniper. During the five-hour NRA-sponsored course, he taught me the fundamentals of marksmanship, operation of semi-automatics and revolvers, and live-fire manipulations. The use-of-force considerations appealed to me most because I refused to be their victim. I needed to learn personal safety, and how to recognize, avoid, and prevent crime. After the course, I felt prepared but wanted enhanced training. To heighten my shooting precision, I took an additional 30 hours of one-on-one lessons with the retired agent on basic carbine operation to prepare me for battle. We focused on shooting positions, optics selection, zeroing and confirmation, target-engagement techniques, speed, and — most importantly — accuracy.

I was ready to engage in their warfare and devised a sensible plan to protect my life. Using their adopted philosophy of get rid of the enemy, I needed to do the same. No longer were they going to mess with my family or create conflict within my family, use friends as decoys to lure me, or scheme to take over my personal assets. In addition to benefiting from my insurance policy, they planned to forge my grandmother's signature on a quit-claim deed, have it notarized by an inside acquaintance to transfer home ownership to Landan in the sum of one dollar. Once the deed was transferred to Landan, he planned to obtain an interest-free mortgage loan and an extended line of credit with a subprime lender in the amount of the triple-inflated home appraisal.

His accountant-friend helped him prepare false promissory notes, fake proof of employment documents and fake finance records to supply to the lender with no intentions on repaying the loan. The profits from the orchestrated scheme, $400,000, would be rerouted into Landan's greedy pockets, redistributing $25,000 to each of the key co-conspirators. My heartless friends planned to evict my grandmother from her home, something they've done before. It was the classic American history story of stealing land from native Americans and making them pay to stay on their own property. I later discovered my conniving uncle played a role in their plan to forge my grandmother's signature. I was not going allow this to happen so he had to go too. In the meantime, I signed the house over to a restricted trust so it could not be touched.

I knew their routines just as they knew mine. After all, we were close friends for many years with daily phone talks. I knew where they all worked, the time they left their homes each morning, their Laundromat days, and addresses to all their secret beaus. I planned to rent a car, sneak to their places, hide in an obstructed area, and wait to use my precision shooting training and attack. One by one, I was going to eliminate the harassment, torture, and greed to take over my possessions. They fooled my family and others close to me; now the tables were turned. However, I still needed to legally obtain a gun license to execute my flawless plan. I had a valid firearm permit from Tennessee but the state did not have reciprocity with South Carolina. I had previously spoken with Mr. Gibson, a close family friend and the mayor in the next town, who had major influence and connections. So I called him again but this time for a different reason.

"Hello."

"Hey, Mr. Gibson, good afternoon, it's Laila. How are you?"

"Hello there, my dear. The old man is doing good. How 'bout yourself?"

"I'm well too, Mr. Gibson. I'm calling you because I need a huge favor."

"OK, what's the favor? What can I do for you?"

"I'm glad you asked, Mr. G. I need your assistance in obtaining my firearm permit."

"Firearm permit? Good heavens. Why would a precious young lady like you need to carry a gun?"

"I just want to feel safe, Mr. G. I think every

single woman living alone should have a firearm in her home and on her person."

"Hmmmm," he mumbled.

"You just never know."

I didn't want to alarm him by telling him the real reason I needed to protect myself. He knew me well and knew as a career chemist I was not going to jeopardize my job and promising future. He called the signing judge of the firearm license to let him know I was his niece of good moral character and to expect my urgent application. Two weeks later, I received the permit in the mail. I then planned to park outside Landan's exclusive gated community home on the hill of suburban Charleston. But when the opportunity finally presented itself, I was too afraid to the pull the trigger. I didn't have the heart. Intentionally killing somebody would practically kill me inside. It's mind-blowing to know people could be so greedy, senseless, and numb to taking the life of another human being. When people are that cold-hearted, they have usually suffered an emotional loss or devastating pain at some point in their life or childhood. To avoid experiencing hurt again, they develop a cold exterior with no sympathy or remorse in inflicting pain to others. This was the facade Landan created. He was an orphan to the streets and under his godfather Nino's guidance, he learned to emotionally detach himself from others. As a young child, he saw many killings, strangulations and executions, and this became his secret way of life.

Since I didn't have the heart to pull the trigger, I went forward with a different plan. Over the last few months I made countless police reports in several municipalities. Since it was third-party harassment, it was challenging to press charges. Because their plots were going to continue, I called three close cousins living in two different states but close enough to get to me in a few hours. I didn't even bother telling my local male relatives as my ex-friends expected me to. I needed urgency and a contingency plan. If my out-of-state family members ever had to drive here to take care of the issue, they would be in and out within minutes without suspicion or notice. I gave them a list of people involved and who to hold responsible if I ever came up hurt, missing or dead. If that indeed happened, they knew to handle it. They were furious about the details and wanted to drive to Charleston immediately. I had them hold off and only react if they didn't hear from me as daily scheduled.

Landan heard a list existed from another unsuspecting close friend of mine but he thought my cousin Stan had the list. My out of state cousins and I developed a check-in system to touch base every day by a specified time. If we didn't make contact, they knew something was possibly wrong. One day I was so swamped with work and failed to check in. Immediately they called other family members to learn my whereabouts. The plan also included hearing my voice. Verbal confirmations from other family members were not acceptable. We also created safe codes. One secret word represented I was all right, the bluff code represented imminent danger and the need to react right away, starting with the person on top of the list. To sweeten the revenge, for every person on the list, I added one or two of their close family members since they took such joy in tormenting mine.

The tormentors discovered there was a list with names and bullied Stan into advising me to only give the list to him. To make them think so, I agreed. I never gave Stan the written list nor intended ever to do so because he wasn't the killer-type. I did, however, tell him some of the names over the phone but not all. I gave him just enough information to feed to the assailants but knew enough not to tell him everything. My out-of-state cousins called many times to receive the completed list with names, addresses, alternative addresses and photos of each person. My cousins were anxious and called several times for the list because I was late getting it to them since I didn't know all their addresses off hand. I was running out of time before their next planned attack.

I knew how to get to my friends' homes but never knew their addresses by heart so I left work early, rented a modest car and dashed to Landan's gated community three towns over. I jotted down his address then raced to Gina's run-down city five miles away to add her address, work address, and car description to the list. I added other surprising names to the list including Brent's since he originally hired Caleb to date me in retaliation for me allegedly smashing his storefront and home windows. I intentionally left Tabatha off the list. Even though she's messy and a busybody, a part of me felt bad for her. The fact that Landan and her other so-called friends manipulated and used her as their scapegoat, mouthpiece and cat-paw, and will continue to do so, was sufficient cruelty. I mailed separate lists to each of my three cousins in the form of a "guest list" with a large asterisk next to each VIP: Very Intimidating Perpetrator.

Even though I quit my job to terminate the policy, the assailants found out from my male family member who called my job that my employer carried a three-month continuation coverage which I was unaware of. They didn't know I made new changes with an attorney, so they hatched yet another plot. They also sketched out plans to move out of state within the next few months, purchase new homes and boats, and take exotic vacations. They intended to start a new life and live the American dream with their share of my policy, assets and mortgage fraud totaling over one million dollars. I started to ruffle feathers by letting people know what they were up to, and I went to the police and local media. I contacted a news reporter with whom I was connected over the past three years and shared with her the details of the harassment. In the event something ever happened she could run a story and publish my journal as a memoir. A photojournalist she worked with suggested we try to set them up and catch the harassment and attempted kidnapping on video as evidence for the police and part of their investigative report. It was a magnificent idea, but somehow a mole leaked the information and the tormentors decided to temporarily back off to avoid our sting operation. Their determination would cause them to later resume and eventually lead them to my trap.

My former friends and other unsuspecting people close to me were infuriated because I interrupted their future lavish plans, champagne wishes and caviar dreams. They decided to retaliate, but this time in a different way. Previously they just wanted to see me dead. Since their murderous plans repeatedly failed, they focused on trying to publicly crucify my character. Tabatha and Gina should have advised them that I could care less about what people say or think about me. Since I don't allow people or society to define me, they're slander tactic didn't work. They threw darts to put holes in reputation, hoping the people who respected me would form an adverse opinion and hang my name. My success, my career, and my lavish lifestyle intimated them and reminded them of what they could have been. They were my silent enemies. They despised me and the ground I walked on, and Landan was still angered by my rejection of him and wanted to punish me for making him feel unwanted. Their attempts to assassinate my character didn't work, their rumors about me didn't work, and Caleb and Brent's anonymous calls to child protective services also didn't work. They even orchestrated to plant narcotics in my car. Relentlessly they tried, and repeatedly they failed. This time to get back at me they plotted to turn on Gina.

Since the public rivalry between Gina and me

was still fresh, they plotted against her, knowing most people and the authorities would immediately view me as the prime suspect. They manufactured a plan to kidnap and kill her, and plant evidence in my car and home to frame me for her disappearance and brutal death. Landan forced Tabatha into going along with the plan. Just as I suspected, Landan continued to manipulate and use her as his puppet and loyal pawn. If she refused to participate in their plan, she would become the next victim. She was regretful for ever getting involved from the beginning because it didn't feel good for her to now be under the heel of their boot. Tabatha was devastated and pleaded to Landan,

"This isn't right, we can't do this?" she cried.

"We have to get this bitch, and this is the best way."

"I can't go along with this LJ. You're going way too far."

"Tabatha, stop fucking crying and suck that shit up. Stop being a fucking punk. Where's your loyalty?"

"I'm loyal to both of ya"ll. I can't believe this is happening. Can't we just do something else? Gina's our girl."

"Fuck Gina! She doesn't give a shit about you."

Landan was good at creating conflict between trusted friends, and playing one against the other. He softened her resistance by working on her insecurity and emotions. Although Tabatha was reluctant, she boldly went along with their diabolic plan. They carried on as business as usual with Gina while they worked on mastering their plan all the way to the end. They took into account every possible outcome, consequence and hindrance, and developed contingency plans for every scenario.

All sporting freshly-inked matching Loyalty tattoos, they spent more time with Gina as a group and hung out at her house to get closer to her and her kids. Caleb remained close as his new role was to monitor her movements and learn her daily patterns. They believed people are creatures of habit and follow the same daily regimen. Since Tabatha mastered the artful craft of spying and posing as a friend, her task as the informer remained. As part of the scheme, Landan used generosity to disarm Gina. He gave Caleb cash to purchase decoying gifts for her, just as he gave Arnell cash to purchase lavish, belated birthday gifts for me. Many of the tactics used to manipulate and outmaneuver me, they employed to deceive defenseless Gina.

They also used selective honesty, and shared dark secrets about the other to gain her trust and lower her guard. Their ulterior motives were overshadowed by the clouded smoke of deception. She was too naive to see the truth and blinded by her fascination with charming Caleb. To create the illusion of being inferior to her, they appeared to value her opinion on the abandoned conspiracy to get rid of me. They psychologically used the idea of slaying me to further weaken and manipulate her, and deteriorate her guarded armor. Timing was everything so they didn't want to rush and risk defecting their plan. For the next several weeks they rehearsed their orchestrated plot with sketched-out blueprints to stab yet another devoted friend in the back.

Over lasagna dinner and chilled imported Italian wine from Landan's private wine cellar, they laughed with Gina about the anticipation of torturing and killing me. She had no inclining the plot against me turned on her and she was now their new target. They formed a strategic alliance with her, recruited the same cast of cold-blooded assailants, and misled her into believing she would have the pleasure of seeing me tortured in an old abandoned meat warehouse four blocks from her quiet street. Thinking I would be in the warehouse tied up and dangling from ceiling meat hooks, she enthusiastically accepted the role of throwing the first forceful blow to my head, and agreed to meet LJ and Caleb at the warehouse unarmed in two weeks. She had no idea they planned to lead her to her fate through a thick fog of discord, deception and disloyalty. For the next two weeks, she looked forward to the day.

* * *

SHARI W. QUINN

ABOUT THE AUTHOR

Shari W. Quinn is a native of Albany, New York. After living in suburban Atlanta for eight years, she relocated back to New York's Capital Region. She is a leader in education, a college instructor, and has been in the higher education industry for more than 14 years. She has served as a guest speaker in over 75 high schools throughout New York State.

She earned her Master's degree in Business Administration (MBA) with a concentration in Marketing from the University of Phoenix in Atlanta; a Bachelor's in Marketing and Management from Siena College in Loudonville, New York; and an Associate's degree in Liberal Arts from Hudson Valley Community College in Troy, New York. She has completed more than two years toward her Doctor of Education (Ed.D.) degree in Educational Leadership, and is currently pursuing her doctoral degree with Northeastern University in Boston.

Shari had always wanted to author a book and challenged herself to embark on the journey of fiction writing, which she completed under her own newly formed publishing company, Shari Quinn Publishing.

She is the proud mother of three children, Sharia, Ruffus "Pop" IV, and Malik; has two beautiful grandchildren, Anthony Jr., and DeShari'ay; and lives in upstate New York.

SHARI W. QUINN